Sal Gabrini: For the Love of Gemma

MALLORY MONROE

This novel is a work of fiction. All characters are fictitious. Any similarities to anyone living or dead are completely accidental. The specific mention of known places or venues are not meant to be exact replicas of those places, but they are purposely embellished or imagined for the story's sake. The cover art are models. They are not actual characters.

THE RAGS TO ROMANCE SERIES

STANDALONE BOOKS

IN PUBLICATION ORDER:

1. BOBBY SINATRA: IN ALL THE WRONG PLACES

2. BOONE & CHARLY: SECOND CHANCE LOVE

3. PLAIN JANE EVANS AND THE BILLIONAIRE

4. GENTLEMAN JAMES AND GINA

5. MONTY & LaSHAY: RESCUE ME

6. TONY SINATRA: IF LOVING YOU IS WRONG

7. WHEN A MAN LOVES A WOMAN

8. THE DUKE AND THE MAID

9. BOONE AND CHARLY: UPSIDE DOWN LOVE

10. HOOD RILEY AND THE ICE MAN

11. RECRUITED BY THE BILLIONAIRE

12. ABANDONED HEARTS

13. HOOD RILEY AND THE ICE MAN 2:

JUST WHEN I NEEDED YOU MOST

14. DANIEL'S GIRL:

BRAND NEW VERSION UPDATED AND EXPANDED

MALLORY MONROE SERIES:

THE RENO GABRINI/MOB BOSS SERIES (22 BOOKS)

THE SAL GABRINI SERIES (13 BOOKS)

THE TOMMY GABRINI SERIES (11 BOOKS)

THE MICK SINATRA SERIES (16 BOOKS)

THE BIG DADDY SINATRA SERIES (7 BOOKS)

THE TEDDY SINATRA SERIES (5 BOOKS)

THE TREVOR REESE SERIES (3 BOOKS)

THE AMELIA SINATRA SERIES (2 BOOKS)

THE BRENT SINATRA SERIES (1 BOOK)

THE ALEX DRAKOS SERIES (9 BOOKS)

THE OZ DRAKOS SERIES (2 BOOKS)

THE MONK PALETTI SERIES (2 BOOKS)

THE PRESIDENT'S GIRLFRIEND SERIES (8 BOOKS)

THE PRESIDENT'S BOYFRIEND SERIES (1 BOOK)

THE RAGS TO ROMANCE SERIES (12 BOOKS)

GIRLS ON THE RUN: A GABRINI VALENTINE

BONITA SINATRA: TO CATCH A JOCK (1 BOOK)

STANDALONE BOOKS:

ROMANCING MO RYAN

MAEBELLE MARIE

LOVING HER SOUL MATE

LOVING THE HEAD MAN

TABLE OF CONTENTS

CHAPTER ONE

Three Months Earlier

"Curtis?"

He kept on typing.

"Curtis?"

Still nothing.

She placed the palm of her hand on his desk. "*Curtis*!"

Her loud screech got everybody's attention. Especially Curtis. But her tactic worked. He stopped typing and looked up from his computer screen at the young office clerk standing at his desk. "Yes, Peaches, what do you want?"

"I need to leave early today."

Leave early? *Again*? Was she for real? But if she was so hellbent on hanging herself, why should he have to pull back the rope? "Okay girl."

She smiled. "Thanks, Curtis!" And then she hurried out of the secondary office, where Curtis shared space with three paralegals, and went into the main office up front, where the other office clerks were housed. Curtis shook his head as she grabbed her purse out of her desk drawer and left. Then he resumed his typing.

But Anne, one of the paralegals, still couldn't believe it. "You're letting her get away with that? She just got hired a few weeks ago and she's leaving early again? She left early three times last week, Curtis."

"You know I know it."

"Then why didn't you tell her no?"

"I'm not her keeper. I'm not telling her nothing. I'm gonna let Miss G tell her something. 'Cause what she's gonna tell her is *you're fired*!"

"Sure about that?"

When Curtis and Anne heard that familiar voice, they looked toward their office entrance. And standing there all decked down in Prada head to toe, Curtis noticed, was *Miss G* herself: Gemma Jones-Gabrini. He was shocked. "I didn't hear you walk up, Miss G."

"Why you keep calling her Miss when you know she's not single, Curtis?"

"Why should she care what I call her? She don't care nothing about what I call her. Do you, Miss G?"

Gemma did, but she wasn't going to let either one of them distract her from her point. "I saw how you handled that young clerk. Don't let it happen again."

Curtis frowned. "Don't let what happen again?"

"Don't let Peaches leave early again," said Anne.

"Don't sabotage her," said Gemma.

12

"You talk to her. You teach her. She's young and dumb just like every last one of us used to be at some point in our lives. Warn her, yes. Write her up if you have to. But don't sabotage the child, Curtis."

Curtis flapped his hands in his limp-wrist, *whatever* way. "She's sabotaging herself if you ask me," he said.

"I'm not asking you," Gemma made clear. "I'm telling you to do your job and help her to understand the ramifications of her actions. You're her supervisor, which at this firm means you teach more than you punish. Understood?"

Gemma could tell he was pissed. And although she gave him more liberties than most around the firm, he knew her well enough to know there were lines she wasn't going to let even him cross. Disobedience was one of those lines.

Curtis was pissed. She was right about that. But he was nobody's fool. "Yes, ma'am," he said. "I will help her to the very best of my ability. It shall become my life's work to help our sweet little innocent Peaches as much as I possibly can."

Gemma couldn't suppress a smile. "You are such a liar," she said, and everybody in that office laughed.

But Gemma knew she got her point across. She looked at her paralegal. "Anne, pull the Granger file for me please. I need a refresh on Day 3 witness testimonies."

"Do you want me to just pull Day 3 witness notes, or the whole thing?"

"Bring the entire case file."

"Yes, ma'am," Anne said as she hurried into the file room.

"And Curtis," Gemma added with a point of her finger.

"Yes ma'am?"

"Behave."

"Who me?" Curtis had a smile on his face and his hand over his heart. "When on earth do I not?"

Gemma smiled too, and left. She and Curtis had a bond, but within limits.

But by the time Anne had grabbed the case record and was coming out of the file room, Curtis was looking out of the window. "Uh-oh," he said.

"Uh-oh what?"

"Boss Man just drove up. With his little racist ass."

Anne looked where Curtis was looking.

"I don't know how racist he is," said Anne, "but he sure is fine."

"He's trying to look all professional in those double-breasted suits when he looks like the stereotypical mobster if there ever was one."

Anne smiled again. "If mob looks like him then I want some of that! And why you always calling him *Boss Man* like he's some *massa* on a plantation?"

"Because that's exactly how he acts with

his mean ass. Always cracking the whip. He says frog. We all say how high. Including Miss G."

"That's not even true and you know it," Anne said as she began heading out of their office. "You're confusing Mrs. Gabrini with your boy Robby Yale. Now that's an ass that be jumping all over the place when Mr. Gabrini shows up," she added with a laugh.

"Keep Robby out of this," she could hear Curtis say as she walked out of the office. But she slammed the door before he could finish.

"You know you heard me heifer!" she also heard Curtis say. She laughed as she made her way to Gemma's office.

The law firm was expanding by leaps and bounds, but it was still The Gemma Jones Firm no matter how many top tier lawyers they acquired. And it was Anne's pleasure to be her para. She knocked once at the boss's office door, and then walked on in.

Gemma was seated behind her desk,

watching her baby girl from her desk computer screen. Her husband had cameras installed all over the house after the baby was born, which gave them full access to check on her twenty-four-seven. And Gemma was constantly checking. The baby, on this check, was in the nursery at home and her two nannies had her laughing so hard at their funny faces that they had Gemma laughing too.

Five months ago she delivered a healthy baby girl. Gemma like Sal select the name, and he selected a doosy. Teresa Alexandria Gabrini was her name. She had her father's big, bright green eyes and her mother's velvety smooth dark skin. She was strikingly beautiful even as an infant. Having her as part of the family was a shot in the arm for her, Sal, and their oldest son Lucky too. He was a great big brother. But he and Sal were spoiling her rotten already. But Gemma didn't mind. She knew how to rein it in. She knew Tee, like Lucky, would turn out just fine.

"Your husband is here," Anne said as she made her way to Gemma's desk. "I would ask if you would like for me to bring him back, but he always comes back without bothering to get permission anyway."

"And so he should," Gemma pointed out, defending Sal. "He's the one who bankrolled all of this."

But that was confusing to Anne. "Why would a successful lawyer need her husband to bankroll her business?"

"Because I wasn't always successful. Not by a longshot."

There was a time, when she first met Sal, that she had such a losing record as an attorney that few would hire her. Her law practice was on life support. Sal, with his connections, and Reno Gabrini, who actually gave her her first big break, brought it back to life. But none of her employees understood Sal at all. To them he was just this mean, bossy, white guy Mafia type who they didn't feel deserved a kind sister like Gemma Jones. But for Gemma, it was the other way around. She was the one who felt fortunate to have a good man like Sal in her corner.

Within seconds after Anne had left Gemma's office, Sal Gabrini, the head of the Gabrini crime syndicate and the second most powerful mob boss in the world, was walking through her door like the mean-looking, bossy white guy Mafia type her staff took him for. Gemma smiled. He closed the door behind him.

"Hey babe," she said as he began walking toward her desk. Something about Sal always gave Gemma a boost when he walked in. And it wasn't because he was some smiley, happy guy. That was so not Sal. But he made her feel happy inside. "What's that?" she asked him as she looked down at the small tote bag he was carrying.

"I got you some lunch."

"Oh thanks. What is it?"

"Lobster Gnudi."

"Oh Sal!" Gemma happily jumped up from behind her desk and made her way toward him. She loved that dish!

"Now she comes running. She comes running for the food," Sal said as Gemma laughed and threw her arms around him. "Wasn't jumping up and running when it was just my ass."

But he was so happy to feel his wife in his arms again that he closed his eyes as he held her. Even though he knew the lunch had the edge on her true affections.

When they stopped embracing, Sal took his free hand and squeezed Gemma's tight ass with a tight squeeze. And he didn't release it, which was a come-on for Gemma.

They leaned back and looked into each other's eyes. Sal's were tired and green. Gemma's were big, bright, and brown. "Thank you, Sal Luca for going out of your way to get me my favorite meal. You're a sweetheart, you know that? Just a loveable teddy bear. I see why Tee's always happy when she sees you."

Sal inwardly smiled just thinking about their brand-new baby girl. But he wasn't going to reveal that to Gemma. "If you ever call me a teddy bear around any one of my men, including Robby Yale, I'll kick your ass."

"Why kick it," Gemma quickly fired back, "when you can always kiss it?"

Sal smiled. That was what he loved about Gemma above any other woman on the planet. She didn't play games. She said what she meant and meant what she said. And just looking at her and her smooth, dark skin and her sweet, soft eyes, and the way her tight ass felt as he squeezed it, did if for him.

He kissed her. Sweetly and lovingly at first. He always loved her taste. But it was that taste that broke him and he began kissing her so passionately that he was sitting that bag of food on her desk and backing her against the wall.

As she ran her hands through his hair as they continued to kiss wildly, he was pulling down the panties beneath her skirt, unbuckling and unzipping his pants and dropping them to his ankles along with his briefs. Then he unbuttoned her blouse, lifted her bra, and moved his lips from her mouth to her breasts. Her head leaned back as he began sucking her, lifting her up, and squeezing her bare ass with a roughness Gemma loved. And when he entered her, she let out such a loud, guttural groan that Sal had to cover her mouth with a kiss so they wouldn't be heard.

They were in sync from the very beginning. Both of them were moving in a groove that had Sal sliding so deep into Gemma that he knew he was hitting her exactly where she loved being hit. And she always moved so tight around his thick penis that it felt as if it could barely move. Something about sex with the one you loved captivated both of them. All they wanted was each other.

All they wanted was to stay where they were: him deep inside of her gyrating his ass off.

And when they came, they came together. It was an exhilarating feeling. They both were buckling to the furiousness of those feelings. They both were trying hard as they could not to scream out in euphoria. But they were moaning. They were enjoying every second as Sal couldn't stop pouring into her and she was wrapping herself so completely around him that it was Sal's muscular body, rather than that wall, holding her up.

And when it was all over and Sal had no more to give, he gave up. He kissed her for several seconds on the lips, rested against her even longer, and then pulled out of her with a slow, very long, very tender pull out.

Then he looked at her and smiled. The lines of age began to appear on the corners of his tired eyes. "Not bad," he said.

"Not bad? You've had better?"

He wanted to say *every day of the week*

23

just to needle her, but he couldn't even lie. "Not a chance," he said, and they kissed again.

And then, after they both realized they had jobs and couldn't stay where they were all day long, he carried her into her ensuite bathroom, sat her on the countertop, and cleaned her up. But as she watched Sal clean himself up, her iPhone started ringing. She jumped off of the vanity, hurried out of the bathroom, and grabbed her phone off of her desk. When she saw that it was Rick Mulganis, a seasoned, veteran attorney she hired a few years back to assist with all of her firm's cases that were up for appeal, she quickly answered. He had been waiting for the appeals court to issue their ruling on one particular case she had worked so hard. "What happened?"

"They just published it."

"And?"

"We lost the appeal, Gem."

Gemma let out a big exhale. She went

from elation with Sal, to this. "Damn!"

"They upheld the lower court with a stinging rebuke of our case. This is going to destroy Donte."

Gemma shook her head and squeezed the bridge of her nose. "It's going to destroy Miss Bettye too."

Miss Bettye, Donte's mother, was a longtime employee of Gemma's firm. Because of the sensitivity of their materials, they didn't hire agency workers. They had their own cleaning crew. His mother was one of the maids on that crew. It was because she personally asked that Gemma agreed to take on the case of her son pro bono. And give it all she had.

"Let's hope Archie can keep her from totally falling apart," Rick said. "Want me to drop by the house and tell her and Archie the unfortunate news?"

"No, I'd better do it. I don't know if you'll be able to handle their reaction because it's going to be devastating. It was just the three of them. Now it's just the two of them."

"Didn't she say she had a doctor's appointment today anyway?"

"She said she'd be home after lunch. She said she was too nervous sitting around the house waiting to hear the news."

"Poor lady. She doesn't deserve this. But this ruling is out of this world, Gem. According to the appeals court, we were idiots for even bringing a case. They said the lower court judge was right to deny our request for reconsideration, and we should have ended it there. They wrote the opinion as if there were no errors during his trial at all, and that Donte got exactly what he deserved. The evidence, they said, was overwhelming. They had the nerve to write that even if there had been some prosecutorial misconduct, it paled against the evidence. *Paled against it*, they said, as if our system of jurisprudence meant nothing to them."

"It doesn't mean shit to them if it's the prosecution's office that's misbehaving," said Gemma. "They always err in favor of the State unless it's so obviously egregious that they have no choice. But you go pay Donte a visit. Explain everything to him. He was so hopeful. As was I."

"Okay, boss. I'll get over there now. See you later on." And Gemma ended the call.

"What was that about?" Sal asked as he entered the office zipping his pants. "Got another cock-sucking crook off scot-free?"

"Just the opposite," said Gemma. Then she shook her head. "Three losses in a row. First Braddock. Then Frazier. Now Donte. That may be a record for me. My firm is on a winning streak. But me personally? I haven't had a win in nearly two months."

Sal placed his hands in the pants pockets of his double-breasted suit and looked at her. He could feel her disappointment. "You okay?"

"I'm okay. Was just hoping for a different outcome. Especially for Donte. He seems like such a good kid."

"You figured he was innocent, hun?"

"I don't know about that! There was a lot of evidence against him, but we had some good points too. But his mother was convinced he was framed."

"Framed?" Sal scoffed. "He was guilty as sin if that's the defense. Framing somebody ain't as easy as people think it is. I should know."

Gemma never liked Sal talking so flippantly about that very messy side of his life. She was law and order and believed in the rule of law. He believed in frontier justice: *You do it to me, I'm going to do it to you and do it to you even worse*.

She began to go into her lunch bag. "This meal you were sweet enough to bring to me will surely help."

"Good. But I gotta go. I'm already late."

"Nobody forced you to stay here."

"Like hell! You absolutely forced me. Those big browns of yours took one look at what I'm packing and I couldn't get your horny ass off of me."

Gemma laughed. "Boy bye!" she said as she tried to hit him across his ass, but he scooted up and she missed.

"And remember it's movie night tonight," she reminded him. "You'd better be home in time, Sal Luca."

"I'm always home in time. It might be late time, but it's still time," he added with a grin, and then he left the office.

Gemma leaned her head back, all smiles gone, as she thought about Miss Bettye. But those were the breaks. Getting slapped with those kinds of rulings was the absolute downside to being a defense attorney.

But Sal was her saving grace. She opened up that container and started chowing down.

CHAPTER TWO

It was late afternoon by the time Gemma's Bentley drove onto the driveway of the small, clapboard house on Durham Street. She got out with her keys and her phone and rang the bell only once before Archie's voice came over the Ring doorbell intercom. "Hey, Miss Jones. The door's open. Come on in!"

Although she introduced herself to all of her clients as Mrs. Gemma Jones-Gabrini, most could only remember the Gemma Jones part. It used to annoy the heck out of Sal. He wanted his wife to be referred to as Mrs.

Gabrini. Mrs. *Sal* Gabrini even better. But they were both used to it now.

"We're back here," Archie yelled out as Gemma entered the small home. Well-familiar with the house after dropping by so many times to discuss Donte's case, she made her way to where she knew Archie would be: in their little game room playing one of his video games. He was a college kid, but he was still a kid.

Archie sat his game controller down and hurried over to the door as she entered the game room. "I hope it's good news," he said anxiously. "Tell me it's good news, Miss Jones. Please tell me it's good news."

"Is your mother here?"

"No ma'am. She's still at the doctor's."

"I thought you said *we* were back here?"

"Just a habit. Mama always saying it that way to make people think there's more than just her at home at all times. I started doing it too. But is it good news?"

Gemma could tell he already knew it

wasn't. She would be smiling if it was good news. She wasn't smiling at all. "No, Archie. Unfortunately, it's not good news. The appeals court affirmed the conviction."

"Ah man!" He was devastated. Then he shook his head. She could see tears begin to form in his eyes. He looked at her. "Donte know?"

"He's being notified as we speak." Then Gemma squeezed his broad shoulder. "I'm so sorry, son. I know how much you wanted your little brother to come home to you and Miss Bettye."

"How can they do that to him though? He didn't kill nobody! It's gonna destroy mama." Tears were falling down his face. "It's gonna destroy her, Miss Jones."

Gemma grabbed the young man and comforted him with a big bear hug. She'd known both boys for years, when Miss Bettye first started working for her and the boys, when they were younger, would come to work with

32

her to help her out. Gemma, who used to work very late, admired their strong work ethic. She grew quite fond of both brothers. When Archie got his full football scholarship to attend UNLV, she was elated for him. But Donte chose a different path. It broke her heart when Miss Bettye told her about his arrest for murder.

"You've got to be strong for your mother," Gemma was telling Archie. "She's really going to need you when she's told."

But as she held the young man and talked to him, comforting him, she could feel a change in his energy. At first he felt slumped into her arms, as if he was destroyed just like she knew he would be. But then he began to stand taller, as if he was enjoying her embrace. And before she knew it, she could feel his expanding penis against her thigh.

As soon as she felt his arousal, she quickly tried to stop embracing him. But as soon as she tried to break away, he pulled her against his body even closer and started looking suggestively at her lips. Then his grip tightened even more around her and he was kissing her with a hot, hard kiss that felt nothing like Sal's kisses. She was so stunned that she managed to push him away from her with a violent push. "What's wrong your ass?" she said to him angrily. "I know you're upset about your brother but I'll be damn if you come at me like that. You know better than that, Archie!"

"I don't know shit," Archie said, looking menacing to her now. "All I know is my brother's gone away for life and they're throwing away the key. That's all I know!" he said angrily and grabbed her again and then flung her onto the sofa in the game room. Then he jumped on top of her.

Gemma wasn't just angry anymore. He was scaring her now. This kid she used to give bubble gum to was trying to assault her? *Seriously*? She was kicking and screaming from the top of her lungs and clawing his face like it was a scratch board.

But he was too big for her. He overpowered her easily. And when he ripped her panties off of her, and then entered her before she realized he had even pulled down his shorts, she was fighting for her life. But he was so big that not even her wrists were moving. She was completely pinned down by his big, defensive-tackle-body.

Gemma was in stunned disbelief. She knew this kid! It was Miss Bettye's oldest boy. A good college kid on his way to bigger and better things. His future was as bright as the sun. And he was doing this shit to her? He was doing this shit to the wife of Sal Gabrini, a man even he had to know was reputed to be a notorious mob boss. *Was he insane*?

He apparently was because he was pumping on her hard and painfully. But thankfully, he was lousy at it. It was all over in less than a minute. His release was so nothing that she didn't even feel it. Sal would pour into her for what seemed like days. Even after showering she would still have his cum inside of her. This fool, fortunately, was no Sal. He sucked at it. Yet he was groaning as if it was the best fuck he'd ever had.

But when he was done, he changed again. He leaned up and looked into Gemma's face and then seemed to suddenly realize that he had just made the worst decision of his entire life. He was no longer the menacing attacker. He was the young man that used to grin when she gave him bubble gum. But now, realizing what he'd done, he was as scared as she had been.

And Gemma took advantage of that weakness and was finally able to push his big-ass body off of her.

"I'm so sorry, Miss Jones," he was saying as he cried. "I didn't mean to do it. I was just angry at what happened to my baby brother. I'm sorry Miss Jones!"

She couldn't believe he thought sorry

was going to cut it. But she didn't care if he was or not. It was her time to rain down some fear on him. And she didn't hesitate. She started punching him with her fist in such a fast, angry way that all he could do was roll up into a ball and take it. Then she grabbed anything she could get her hands on. She grabbed his game controller first, and slammed it upside his head repeatedly until it broke in two.

"I didn't mean it, Miss Jones," he was still crying. "I didn't mean it!"

Then she grabbed the computer on the table next to the sofa and started slamming it upside his head too, breaking the top from the bottom of that computer too. She was hitting him so hard that he fell off the sofa.

"I never done anything like that before," he was crying. "I didn't mean it!"

But Gemma wasn't trying to hear his cries. She started kicking him and stomping on him with her four-inch heels and yelling angrily

37

at him as she did. "You asshole!" she yelled. "Fuck you, you bastard!"

"Please, Miss Jones, don't tell Mama." He was desperate. "You can't tell my mama. I'm all she's got now. It'll kill her if you tell."

He was acting as if he touched her ass or stole a kiss from her. "You raped me!" she screamed. "You raped me you pile of shit! You raped me!"

And she wouldn't let up. She kept on kicking him and stomping him until he was almost unconscious. "You fool," she was now yelling as she stomped, her words mixed with hatred and disappointment. "My husband will kill you if he finds out!"

And she wasn't just whistling Dixie either. Sal would crush this kid to death with his bare hands if he ever found out. But Archie wasn't whistling Dixie either. Miss Bettye, Gemma knew, would die if she knew what Archie had done to her employer. Archie, even above Donte, was her pride and joy. He was the family's leader. He was their golden ticket out of lifelong poverty and struggling. For literally one minute of stupidity, he had just thrown his mother to the wolves, and thrown his great future on the trash heap.

"You stupid fool!" Gemma said angrily as she stomped him in the face again, this time barely missing his eye.

"I didn't mean it, Miss Jones," he kept saying as he rolled into a fetal position, and cried like a baby.

But no innocent would do what he did, and Gemma knew that. On no day could anybody confuse her as a weakling. And on any other day she would be calling 911 right then and there. She would be waiting for the cops to come and get his ass. But it was complicated. It was crazy complicated!

She stood there, breathing heavily after such a vengeful retaliation, and her heart was heavy with emotion. How could he be so stupid? How could he so callously risk, not just his future, but his beloved mother's very life?

But Gemma wasn't going to stand there and ponder it. He made his bed.

She grabbed her ripped panties and her car keys and hurried out of that house like she was getting out of Dodge. She used to enjoy coming to their home. It always felt so warm and inviting. Now it felt like a grave.

CHAPTER THREE

She drove around Vegas for what seemed like several hours. She couldn't stop herself from crying and then becoming so angry that she was hitting the steering wheel with the palm of her hand. She was so torn with competing emotions that it felt as if she was going to explode. Why hadn't she called 911 already? What was her damn problem?

Reality was her damn problem. Beyond the anger and the incredible violation, she had to face the facts.

She was a longtime lawyer who defended many rape cases in her day. She knew it would be his word against her word and it would be an uphill battle all the way. Especially if he was the athlete his mother claimed he was because she knew all those vultures who would stand to profit mightily from his entrance into the NFL draft and ultimately into the NFL would pay dearly for the best lawyers in the country to defend his case. And they would rip her to shreds. They would claim it was all consensual. Two adults doing what adults did. She would claim it wasn't consensual at all, but was outright rape, and she would show her torn panties to prove it. But the defense would claim she ripped those panties herself. Why on earth would she rip her own panties, she would ask. And their response would be the same response she used to give when defending her clients accused of rape: Because she wanted this fine specimen of a football player, a soon-to-be NFL lottery pick, for herself. As her young boy toy.

And his lawyers wouldn't stop there, because she wouldn't if he were her client either. They would claim she and Archie were fooling around long before the day of the assault, but Archie was just using her to keep her working hard for his brother. His lawyers would claim that after the appeal failed, he dumped her like a bad habit. He got one last hit off of her, and then told her he didn't want to be bothered with her anymore. And that, his lawyers would claim, was when she, as a woman scorned, concocted the rape story.

But that nightmare scenario would only occur if the case ever went to trial. Because there wouldn't even be a trial when Sal found out. He would become Archie's judge, juror, and executioner that very night. It would be the end of the family dream of getting out of poverty. It would be the end of Miss Bettye, too, with both of her boys gone forever. Gemma knew there was no way that old lady would survive a day if she lost both of her boys.

She slammed her hand against the steering wheel again as she drove. Because she had to make a decision. Tell it all and let the chips fall where they may. Or keep it to herself, and herself alone, and let Miss Bettye have at least one of her sons to make her proud. Because if she told anybody, including her best friend Trina, she would get no relief. Trina and everybody else in the family would insist on retribution. And not the kind Gemma had already meted out either. They would want Archie Jefferson dead. It would be hands down unanimous. Give Miss Bettye some money if it would make you feel better, they would tell her, but get rid of that sonofabitch without delay.

That would be easy for them to say, Gemma knew, because Miss Bettye was just a name to them. Just a face they may or may not have seen around the law firm. Because if they truly knew her, they knew she wouldn't accept a dime from Gemma. She was a strong, hardworking, proud black woman. Money would be the last thing she wanted. She'd just want her boys back.

It wasn't an easy decision for Gemma.

She was more than just a name to Gemma.

But she had to make a decision. She had to go all in, because Sal and the other Gabrinis and Sinatras too would go all in once they found out. Or she had to keep that shit to herself. And herself alone.

But what if he did it to somebody else? What if this wasn't just a lapse in judgment like it seemed to be to Gemma? She didn't know what to do! She just wanted to go home. To think.

But just as she was driving by her law firm, which she had to drive by to get home, she suddenly slammed on brakes, did a U-turn, and sped into her parking lot. Because there, in her parking lot, was an ambulance and many of her attorneys and front office workers standing outside. As she was getting out of her Bentley, Curtis hurried over.

"What's going on, Curt?" She kept walking toward the ambulance.

Curtis was walking with her. "It's Miss

Bettye."

Gemma looked at him. "Miss Bettye? She's here?"

"She had that community transport van drop her off over here from her doctor's office. She wanted to know what was going on with Donte's case."

When Gemma saw Miss Bettye lying in that ambulance, her thin, dark face nearly covered in an oxygen mask, tears still streaming down her face despite her condition, her heart sank. "She knows?" Gemma asked Curtis.

"She wanted answers, so yeah, one of the senior lawyers told her that Donte lost his appeal. And Boss, you should have seen Miss Bettye. She just collapsed and cried out in unbearable pain. We thought somebody was killing her. Then she started clutching her heart, like she was having a heart attack I tell you, and we were all so afraid that I called 911. The poor lady needed serious help. She's in a bad state, Boss."

Gemma was so thrown she could hardly believe it. If Donte losing his appeal would do that to her, she could only imagine what losing Archie to the kind of death he would suffer would do. It would kill her just like Archie said. Just like that asshole said.

"Miss Gemma?" It was one of the paramedics on scene. He was peering out of the back of the ambulance. "Is there a Miss Gemma here?"

"Yes," said Curtis as he and Gemma hurried over to the ambulance.

"I'm Gemma."

"The lady here wants a word," the paramedic said and then helped Gemma up into the ambulance. They were still hooking Miss Bettye up to various tubes and drips.

"You're going to be just fine, Miss Bettye," Gemma said.

But Bettye took her hand. "Promise me you'll go to Archie and tell him what happened

47

with Donte. Don't let nobody else tell him. I want you to tell him. You'll comfort him. You'll look out for him."

Gemma was alarmed as she said those innocent words. After the ordeal she'd just been through, they sounded almost terrifying to Gemma.

"You hear me, Miss Gemma? Please be with Archie. He'll need you when he finds out the fate of his baby brother. And please don't tell him I'm at the hospital. That'll just add to his worries. I'm all he's got now, and he's all I got. Please be there for him."

Gemma wanted to throw up. She felt just that ill. There was no way she was going anywhere near Archie Jefferson ever again! But there was no way she could say no to his sweet, kind mother. "I'll handle it," was all she was able to say.

It was enough. Miss Bettye squeezed her hand even as the paramedics were telling Gemma she had to get out so they could leave.

But when Gemma stepped out of that ambulance, that small meeting with Miss Bettye only crystallized everything for her. And she had to get real. Because she was more convinced now than ever that if she told what happened in that game room, she wouldn't just be signing Archie's death warrant, but Miss Bettye's death warrant too.

She could never harm, nor cause to be harmed, that wonderful, hardworking, kind and selfless lady.

CHAPTER FOUR

Movie night in Sal and Gemma's backyard. The big screen was up and Salvatore Luciano Gabrini, Junior, called Lucky or Lucci to everybody who knew him, was back there with one of his friends, a cute blonde he was trying out to see if she would measure up to the kind of lady worth his time. His father Sal was out there too, holding baby Teresa and making her grin with his various facial expressions. The movie, on a streaming channel, was going through the usual *coming soon* commercials. But not for much longer.

"Where's Ma?" Lucky asked his father. "The movie's about to start."

Sal looked around. He was so busy playing with Teresa that he didn't realize Gemma had not made it outside yet. He handed the baby to Lucky. Lucky nor the baby seemed to mind being suddenly thrust upon each other, as they both started smiling at each other. And Sal went inside looking for Gemma.

Lucky's girlfriend was staring at his baby sister. "She's so black," she said with a grin, as if being black was a crime.

Lucky looked at her. "What do you mean?"

"Compared to us," the blonde said, still smiling, "she's so black."

"But what's that supposed to mean?"

The girl, suddenly realizing she had revealed too much of the negative side of herself when she was determined to be all positive to win the best catch around, tried to backtrack. "It means nothing at all, Lucky. What I meant to say is that she's so pretty. Isn't she? She's black, but she's pretty. I mean, she's black *and* she's pretty. That's what I meant to say."

But the handsome, popular, muscular

young man was staring at her. He was a
quarterback. He was the captain of the
baseball team too. His stock and trade was
sizing up his opponent quickly, and then
making a decision. Quickly. "I think you
should leave," he said to his date. With her
few words, she'd already shown him what she
was about.

But the girlfriend was mortified. She
had already bragged incessantly to her friends
about how she was going on a date tonight
with Lucky Gabrini, and that she just might
meet his parents! And she'd blown it already?
"I was just playing around," she said with an
even bigger smile. "You know me. Always the
kidder. Of course she's black. Her mother's
very black. Why wouldn't she be black? I
didn't expect her to be so black, given that her
father's white, but that doesn't mean she's not .
. . I mean, she's so pretty. That's what I've
been saying all along. She's so pretty!"

"I'm no longer thinking you should

leave," Lucky said calmly. Then he gave her a look that brook no compromise. "Leave," he ordered.

The girlfriend knew that look. He gave it to his opponents on the football field. Now he was giving it to her. She was angry, and hurt, and super-embarrassed, but she got up and left.

Lucky watched her leave. But he felt no remorse. He, instead, looked at his beloved baby sister. "That's right, Gorgeous," he said to her. "Take it from your big brother: Never waste your time on the bullshitters. You hear me? When they show their ass, show them the door. You hear me, girl? Don't waste time. It's too precious."

And then Teresa, as if on cue, started grinning, which lifted Lucky's spirits immediately.

Inside their home, their mother was upstairs in the shower again. And she was crying again. Ever since she made it home and upstairs out of earshot and eyeballs of her family, she was in tears. She couldn't stop herself from crying. And scrubbing off herself once again as if what Archie had done to her was seared onto her skin. She was scrubbing hard.

But when she heard Sal's voice calling her name as he walked up the stairs, she quickly wiped her tears away and steeled herself again.

"Gemma!" he yelled.

"I'm in the shower, Sal!"

"The shower?" Sal made his way through their bedroom and into the ensuite bathroom. He walked over to the shower stall and opened the frosted door with a frown of confusion on his face. "What are you doing in the shower again? This makes what? The third time?"

"It's been a long day, that's all."

"And that's why we're outside watching

a movie under the moonlight. It's time to relax. Come on now."

"I know. I'm coming."

But Sal had a problem. Namely Gemma was naked in front of him and his penis was reacting. In a major way.

And soon he was naked himself, and in that shower with Gemma. And he had her hands splayed against the shower wall as he fucked her long and hard.

Gemma closed her eyes and endured it more than she enjoyed it. Because she couldn't shake what happened in that game room. Earlier that day, after the ambulance left her office, she went to her doctor's office and asked him to check her for any STDs. She knew Doc assumed it was because she suspected Sal of doing something. He wasn't immune to the rumors about her husband and other women. But if he only knew why she was truly there!

Fortunately, the blood tests at the onsite

lab came back negative for any diseases. Because if she didn't have those results, she would not have let Sal anywhere near her sexually.

But she allowed him because she had the results. And because she was hoping that Sal doing her the way she loved could help erase the memory of what was done to her by that animal.

But even Sal wasn't capable of that kind of magic trick.

It didn't ease a thing.

CHAPTER FIVE

Three Months Later

Three months later and another night at Sal and Gemma's. This time a cookout that was still jumping even though they'd been at it all day. Now it was nighttime, the massive backyard was lit up with the kind of floodlights seen on football fields, and all of their guests were still having a blast.

Reno Gabrini, along with his oldest son Jimmy Gabrini, and Sal and his big brother Tommy were at the patio table playing cards. Their women, Trina, Grace, and Oprah were in the yard playing tag football, although they sucked at it. Destiny Gabrini, Tommy's daughter, and Sophia Gabrini, Reno's daughter, were over on the tennis courts with their beaus, but both couples were arguing more than they were playing tennis. Neither one of the Gabrini girls' relationships were going well. But that was young love. It was just a matter of time, Reno figured, before they were both single again.

Lucky and Reno's youngest son Carmine, and Tommy's top-jock son TJ, were out on the basketball court having a blast too. They were furthest away, but you could still hear them talking smack.

But nobody was talking more smack than Reno and Sal.

"Quit cheating, Sal," Reno complained.

"Why am I cheating all of a sudden? Because I'm winning? Because your ass losing?" Then Sal revealed his hand and racked up more chips. "Cheat on that, motherfucker!" he proclaimed, as he and Jimmy high-fived.

"That's how you do that shit, Uncle Sal," Jimmy said with a grin.

Reno rolled his eyes. "Just deal the

cards," he said to his son, whose turn it was to deal. Jimmy, Sal, and Tommy laughed.

"Sore loser," added Sal.

But Reno's attention had already moved away from his losses. He was looking out over the massive backyard to make sure all was well with the family. He could see his daughter Sophie going at it with her beau Von, and Destiny and her old man didn't seem to be on great terms either. Marie, Gemma's biological daughter that Sal adopted, was out there too. She was another young beauty. But she was flying solo that night.

"They going at it, aren't they?" Tommy said, who was looking in the same direction Reno was looking. "But that's young love for you."

"Love my ass," said Reno. "I think Soph's about ready to kick Von to the curb."

"Why? Infidelity?"

"She says he never has time for her. He works too much."

"Welcome to the club. We all work too much, and every one of our wives says so."

"Yeah, but Sophie grew up around that shit. Me and Tree at each others' throats about that every week. Trina would leave, or I would leave. She doesn't want that life for herself. She want better than that. Me and Tree want better for her too."

"Speaking of Trina," said Tommy, looking at their women play tag football. "She seems to be losing like you are tonight."

"Ah fuck you, Tommy," Reno said absently as he looked over at their women. "Look at'em," he said, shaking his head. "They don't know what they're doing." Then he yelled at his wife. "Trina, what are you doing? That's not how you play that game!"

"What you worrying about them for?" asked Sal as he looked over there too. But then he noticed that his wife wasn't among them. "Where's Gemma?" He yelled out to the ladies. "Where's Gemma?"

"She went back inside," said Grace.

"Again? For what?"

"How should we know?" asked Trina. "Throw the ball, Grace!"

Worried, Sal threw his cards in, causing the guys to complain, and got up and went inside his home. He pulled out his phone and pulled up the app for his nursery cameras. Their gorgeous baby girl Teresa was in the nursery asleep in her crib. Her two nannies were quietly talking amongst themselves. But Gemma wasn't in there with them, where Sal thought she might be. But when he walked through the kitchen and then out of the dining hall, he could sense her presence in the living room, although it was pitch black in there. And that sad-ass jazz music she loved playing could be heard over the stereo.

Sal went over and turned on the light in the room. And just as he suspected, Gemma was seated on the sofa, slouched down, her legs crossed, with a glass of champagne in her hand. And as has been the case for months lately, she looked as if she wanted to be anywhere else but where she was.

Sal sat on the sofa across from her. "Hey."

Sal could also tell she didn't like that he had interrupted her flow. But he didn't give a shit. "What's your problem, Gem? You can't speak to people all of a sudden?"

"Sal, I don't want to hear it, okay? I am not in the mood."

"You know what I say to you not being in the mood? Tough. Get in the fucking mood. And then get your ass outside with our guests." He frowned. "What are you sitting up here in the dark for?"

"I'm relaxing, Sal. It's called relaxing."

"It's called bullshit. It's called avoiding shit."

Gemma looked at her husband. She loved him with every fiber of her being, but he just couldn't understand. "What am I avoiding,

Sal?"

"I don't know," Sal admitted. "You won't tell me. But your ass avoiding something."

Gemma shook her head and then leaned it back. "You wouldn't understand."

"Try me. Give me a chance, Gem. I want to understand. Just tell me what's going on with you lately so I can understand."

But like always when it seem as though it could go that deep, something within Gemma rebels, and she comes back up to the surface. "I'm fine, Sal. Stop worrying about me."

"Impossible," said Sal as he sat back on that sofa and cross his legs too, his short pants and tucked-in polo shirt strange to see on him given the double-breasted suits he usually wore. "Telling me not to worry about you when you're in a funk like this is impossible. Telling our baby girl not to cry would be easier."

Gemma stared at him. He was that combination man of strength, but also a man with the kind of sex appeal that women craved and men envied. Whereas his brother Tommy, called *Dapper Tom* for his flawless dress style and looks, was always considered one of the most attractive men of his generation, Sal was among the strongest of his generation. He was a beast in the field when it came to knocking heads and keeping the guys in his syndicate in line.

But there was another side to Sal that none of his men ever got to see. A side reserved exclusively for Gemma. A side that was so fragile and so vulnerable that it alarmed her sometimes. How could he be so tough to the point of pure meanness, and so sensitive too when it came to her, or to their children? But that was precisely why she kept so much bottled up inside. She had to protect Sal. Because she knew him like she knew the back of her hand. If a fellow lawyer were to disrespect her, or some others talked smack to her like they were her equal, she could never tell Sal about any of it. He'd want to kill the offenders, or do so much harm to them that it would put his own freedom in harm's way. And since she knew he would be that aggressive concerning small matters like that, then she was certain he would be out of this world aggressive with bigger matters. Unspeakable matters. Matters that even Gemma couldn't bring herself to face anymore.

"I'm okay, Sal. Alright? I just need a moment."

"You've had moment after moment after moment. We have company outside, Gem. We have people over. Remember?"

"Of course I remember. Do you remember what's in that amusement park of a backyard we have? They have plenty of entertainment back there. They don't need me."

"But I do, Gemma," Sal said heartfelt.

Gemma looked at him. She could just feel his anguish.

"Lucky and Marie and Teresa need you

too," Sal continued. "For their sake, and my sake, you have got to get over whatever this funk is you've been in lately. Or get you some help."

"Don't start."

"I mean it! Who the fuck sits in a dark living room listening to those torch songs like they're home alone somewhere? And I notice you've been on the sauce a little more than usual too lately," he added, looking at that champagne Gemma was drinking. "I'll be damn if I'm going to allow my wife to become a boozer. You ain't forgetting your problems that way. Ain't happening."

Gemma wouldn't allow herself to become an alcoholic either. But he had a point. Sometimes it was easier to lose yourself in a substance. "Go back outside and enjoy yourself, Sal. I'll be back out there soon."

"Nope," said Sal, standing up. "Not soon. Not later. Now. You're going out there now."

"I told you I'll be out there. I just need a little time alone."

"To do what? Sit up in the dark?"

"What difference does it make what I'm doing?" Now Gemma's temper was rising. "I said I'll be out there, Sal."

Sal matched her temper and raised her one. "And I said you're coming out now. Now get your ass up. I'm tired of this shit, Gemma. I'm tired of going around in circles with you!"

"Nobody's forcing you to go around anything with me. I just wanted a little time alone."

"You always want time alone. Every time I turn around, you want time alone. You won't talk to me."

"I do talk to you."

Sat sat back down. Only he sat on the edge of the sofa. "Okay, talk," he said.

But Gemma wasn't about to go there. "There's nothing to talk about."

"See what I mean? It's all bullshit," Sal

said as he stood back up. "Now let's go. I'm not fucking with your ass anymore. Get up."

But Gemma could be as headstrong as Sal. "I told you I'm not going anywhere right now."

"And I told you to get your ass up and let's go outside and enjoy our company. Now let's go," Sal said angrily as he grabbed her by the arm and stood her on her feet.

"Sal stop!" she yelled as her glass of champagne began spilling out. "Look what you did!"

"Then let's go! Put that shit down and let's go, Gemma!"

Outside, Reno was the first to hear the commotion. "What's that?" he asked.

"What's what?" asked Tommy as he threw out another card.

Reno shooshed them. And that was when all of the men at the card table, who were closest to the back patio door, heard the yelling.

"What the fuck?" Reno said as they all jumped up and hurried inside. It sounded as if Sal and Gemma were about to come to blows.

When they got inside, they weren't that far off. Sal and Gemma were in each other's face. "Hey, hey," Reno said as they rushed over and Reno got in between the couple. "What's wrong with you two?"

"I told him I was coming outside later, but he act as if the world will end if I don't go out right this very minute."

"Bullshit!" yelled Sal. "That ain't what this is about. This is about me not wanting you to sit up here in the dark listening to that sad-ass music and drinking yourself into a drunken stupor when you need to be around people."

"Around people," Gemma said, "or around your ass?"

"Both!" yelled Sal, although he was hurt that she would say that as if he was some weak man all in love with her ass. It was true when it came to her. But it was his private

69

truth.

"Just leave me alone, Sal," Gemma pleaded with him. "You aren't hearing me. Can't I just be alone for two minutes? Why do you keep bothering me?"

All the men knew Gemma had crossed a line. You didn't expose a man like Sal's weakness, and especially not in front of men he respected the most. Even though they all already knew Gemma was his weakness, it just wasn't verbalized ever.

And Gemma could see the hurt all over Sal's face. She knew she had crossed the line too. She and Sal stared at each other.

And Sal was done. "Fuck it," he said. "I'll let your ass be alone alright."

"Sal, don't," warned Reno.

"I'll let your ass be alone all night," Sal said and began hurrying toward the front door.

"Uncle Sal!" Jimmy called after him. But once Sal made up his mind, they knew there was no changing it.

Gemma knew it too. But she hurried behind him anyway.

"Let's get back outside, guys," said Tommy.

"I thought they were gonna come to blows," said Jimmy as they began heading back toward the back door.

"Sal wouldn't dare," said Reno.

"Because he wouldn't hit a woman?" asked Jimmy.

"Who wouldn't hit a woman? Let a woman hit me and I'm decking her ass. Same with Sal."

"Then why wouldn't Uncle Sal dare not hit Aunt Gemma?"

"Because he knows if he hit Gemma she'll kick his ass. She's a tough broad, I'm telling you. Not as tough as your mother. She's the champ, unfortunately. She's like Muhammad Ali. But Gemma's tough, too. Like Mike Tyson."

Jimmy laughed. "Oh, Pop, please!"

But Tommy glanced back as they walked away. He knew how hard his brother loved on Gemma. He knew how hurt he was. He was pleased Gemma ran after him. But he was still concerned.

Outside, Sal was making his way toward his Bugatti that was parked, along with their guest cars, in their huge circular driveway. By the time Gemma ran out and caught up with him, he was just opening his car door.

And she didn't beat around the bush. "Sal, I'm sorry," she said. "I didn't mean to hurt you. I was just . . ."

Sal stopped and looked at her. Was she going to actually talk to him this time?

"I'm just . . ." She still couldn't finish the sentence.

"You're just what?" Sal asked her.

But she couldn't go there. She went cliché instead. "Tired. I guess I'm just tired."

Sal stared at her. He couldn't love

anybody more. But sometimes that love scared him. Gemma could really do some serious damage to him if she were to ever wise up and leave his stupid ass. And he was beginning to hate that a human being could have that kind of power over him.

Gemma could see his anguish. She had apparently hurt him more than she had thought. "I'll join the group," she decided to say. "I'll entertain our guests."

"Good," said Sal. "It'll be good for you."

"Let's go out back together. A united front," she said with a smile.

But Sal was already shaking his head. "Nope."

"Why not, Sal?"

Sal looked at her as if she was toying with him. "Why the fuck you think? Talking to me like I'm some little boy in front of Reno and Tommy. You out of your fucking mind?"

Gemma knew he was exaggerating. But she also knew it was how he took it. "I told you I was sorry."

"Sorry didn't do that shit. Your ass did that shit." Then he frowned. "Just go on out back."

"Where are you going?"

But Sal wasn't answering any more questions. He got in his two-million-dollar car, and sped away.

Gemma leaned her head back and then shook it. It would be what she deserved if he went straight into another woman's arms. All of her friends insisted that was what he was doing anyway. All the Gabrini men had mistresses, let the street tell it. But tonight was one of those nights when Gemma didn't just dismiss it. When she wondered, because of all of her own shortcomings, if it was true.

"Great work, Gemma Jones," she said to herself as if she was her own worst critic, and then she did as she promised and headed for the backyard.

But before getting back there, she

calmed her nerves, relaxed herself, and then put on the best smile she could muster as she joined the crowd.

CHAPTER SIX

Early the next morning Lucky got out of bed, went into his ensuite bathroom and peed, and then made his way to the nursery down the hall, to check on his baby sister.

But his mother was already there. He stood in the doorway in his pajamas and leaned against the jamb. Gemma was seated in the rocking chair holding baby Teresa as she rocked her. She was singing softly to her. The two nannies were further over, in the sitting area, having their morning coffee. Lucky glanced at them. But he stared at his mother.

Five months after Teresa was born, he remembered his mother changed a little bit. She wasn't eating right and was working too hard and just didn't seem happy at all to him. That was three months ago. Teresa was now eight months old. And their mother was still in that funk.

But she wouldn't talk about it. She would insist she was okay when even Lucky knew she wasn't. But nobody seemed to know what to do about it.

And his father, who had a bad habit of handling family issues by leaving and going God knows where, wasn't helping at all.

He pushed his muscular body away from the door jamb and walked over to his mother and baby sister. He sat in the chair beside his mother. "You okay, Mommy?"

Gemma's eyes had been closed as she rocked her baby. She was fully dressed and ready for work. Should have left already. But just to hold little Tee and smell her baby scent and just to know what a precious gift God had given to her, eased her mind. She could have stayed there forever. But nothing was forever. "Hey."

"You okay?"

"I'm alright, sure. How are you?"

It was her usual tactic and Lucky knew it like a book. Whereas his father would often leave rather than deal with issues, his mother would often act as if there was no issue to deal with. He knew his parents like he knew his name. "I just woke up. I don't know how I am. I'm asking about you. I'm asking how you're doing."

"Baby, I'm fine. I'm okay."

"Dad okay?"

Gemma didn't answer right away, and that was telling to Lucky too. He stared at her.

Gemma was still pissed with Sal for leaving and not coming back home last night, but that wasn't their son's concern. "He's okay too, baby," she said. "Don't worry about us."

"He didn't come home last night."

Gemma didn't dispute that truth, but she didn't acknowledge it either.

"Carmine said you guys were fighting last night at the cookout. He said you and Pop almost came to blows."

Gemma wanted to kick Carmine's ass. He was always all up in grown folks business. "Why are you always listening to Carmine? You're the leader. All of the young people in the family follow you and Duke. But you follow Carmine!"

"I respect Carmine. He's weird and the kids pick on him because he likes to knit and is always talking that highbrow, out of space shit, but I know for a fact Carmine can kick my ass and Duke's too. Don't get it twisted. He's a certified genius, but he's no nerd." Then Lucky looked at his mother. "And he's no liar either."

"No, he's not," Gemma admitted. "He's a good kid. And I know he's got your back, and you have his."

"That's right," Lucky said, nodding.

"And yes it's true. Your father and I had a bit of a blowup last night. But don't go blaming your father for it."

But Lucky was brutally honest himself. "I blame him for getting so angry that he has to leave to avoid kicking your ass, and then he makes it worse by staying out all night. But I blame you for driving him to it in the first place."

Gemma looked at their beautiful son. He was the spitting image of his father. Whereas Teresa had many of her mother's features, even down to her dark skin tone, Lucky had all of his father's features, even down to his father's white skin tone. But that was a feature of almost all of the Gabrini and Sinatra biracial children: the guys looked white as the driven snow. The girls looked black as black could look. But even though Lucky had the usual Gabrini features, he was heart and soul his mama's boy.

And Gemma smiled and placed her hand on the side of his handsome face. "Hear me well: your father and I are fine. We're going to be just fine. I'm just having a moment, that's all. I don't want you or your sister Marie or anybody else worrying about us. Okay, Lucci?"

Lucky smiled. He was named after his father: Salvatore Luciano Gabrini, Junior. His father nicknamed him Lucky after the way he was kidnapped as a baby and survived that shit. But his mother sometimes called him Lucci Gabrini when she was serious about getting a point across. "You do realize some of the kids in school started calling me Lucci after they heard you call me by that name."

Gemma smiled. "Really?"

"For real though."

"Do you have a preference?"

Lucky thought about it. "I like Lucci because it's more like a play on my middle name. And because Lucky makes me feel like my life it out of my hands. Like I have no control."

"That sounds like something Carmine would say," Gemma said.

Lucky smiled. "It is," he said and they laughed.

Lucky continued. "Carmine said that

there's this guy named J.D. Salinger who wrote in some book that saying good luck to somebody was the worst thing you could say to them. I didn't get it until Carmine explained it to me. It's like luck isn't reliable. It isn't a good thing to lay your hat on. Carmine started calling me Lucci too."

Gemma had never even thought of it that way. "*The Catcher in the Rye*," she said.

Lucky looked at her. "Come again?"

"J.D. Salinger said something to that effect in his novel *The Catcher in the Rye*. I'm sure it was a part of your school's literature curriculum. It was a part of mine when I was growing up."

"I never read it," said Lucky.

Gemma shook his head. "A great American classic and you never read it. What is this world coming to?" she added, with a smile. Lucky had a way of easing her burdens just by hanging around.

But then they both heard the front door

open and just like that Gemma's mood changed right back to melancholy. And she handed the baby to Lucky. "I'd better get going," she said and kissed him on the forehead. "I'll call you." Then she left the nursery.

By the time she made it down the hall and around the corner into their large foyer, Sal was tossing his keys atop the foyer table and about to head further into the house. When Gemma saw him she stopped momentarily, then hurried toward the foyer table to grab her keys on top of the table and briefcase beside the table.

When Sal saw her enter the foyer, his heart began to squeeze. Something about Gemma still made his heart flutter. He looked down the length of her. She was dressed in one of her blue skirt suits, which he knew meant she had be in court this morning. She told him long ago they were taught in law school to wear muted colors during trial or a juror could be turned off. Which made perfect sense to Sal given how stupid some jurors could be. But Gemma wasn't trying to check him out the way he was checking her out. He could tell she was pissed.

But when she grabbed her keys and briefcase and was about to push past him and just leave without saying a word, he grabbed her by the arm and pulled her back toward him. She could smell a combination of his cologne and liquor.

But when he looked into her big, bright eyes, and when she looked into his tired green eyes, all they saw was sadness there. And it was breaking Sal's heart. The look of her, and the sweet, fresh scent of her, made him feel heavy with emotion. He could not love a human being more than he loved his wife, and that fact alone was beginning to scare him. And he had to fight the urge to do what he used to do if some woman got too close to him: sabotage their relationship and force her to leave him. But Gemma wasn't just some woman. If Gemma left him it would kill him. Because he loved her so. And that reality, that she held all the cards over him, was terrifying.

But being in her presence always broke him down. And he could no longer hide his vulnerability. His weakness for her. He leaned in toward her and kissed her on her sweet, tender lips.

Gemma allowed it, which only encouraged Sal to kiss her even more passionately.

She closed her eyes. At first it was painful. She knew Sal cared deeply about her. She knew whenever she hurt, he hurt too. But he wanted her to talk about it when she didn't even know where to begin. But she didn't allow his kiss just because she felt guilty. She allowed his kiss because it was Sal kissing her, the man she loved, and he was taking her to their private, special place once again.

And soon she was returning his passion

and kissing him too. She didn't know where he'd been all night, or who he'd been with, but she was used to that. He never told her where he'd been when he didn't come home. But somehow she trusted Sal. Her friends said she was crazy to trust him. A *gotta have it* man like Sal Gabrini would cheat at the drop of a hat, they said. Even Trina once thought so too and she was married to the King of *gotta have it* Reno Gabrini!

But Gemma knew Sal. She knew he had issues in his past. He used to be a crooked, racist cop back in the day when he and his brother Tommy were actual law enforcement officers. And although he crossed many lines in his line of work, she believed there were certain lines he would never cross no matter what. Gemma believed cheating on her, hurting her, was one of those lines.

When they stopped kissing, they stared at each other again. Both of their hearts were pounding. And then Sal pulled her even closer against him and embraced her with a tight, warm embrace.

Gemma, at first, just stood there. Where were they going with this? She was supposed to be pissed with him. But she'd already kissed him. Now she was allowing him to embrace her too? But those thoughts only lasted a few seconds. Because before she could finish her thoughts, her free hand was embracing Sal right back. He was her weakness too.

But after several more seconds, she pulled back. This was ridiculous! Yes, she was in a bad place last night and he had every right to call her out on it. But he had no right to disrespect their marriage. She couldn't pretend what he did was comparable to the fact that she was in a temporary funk she couldn't get herself out of. There was no comparison.

Sal knew it too. As soon as she pulled back from him, he apologized. Somewhat. "I shouldn't have stayed out all night."

But Gemma wasn't ready to give him any further passes. "You should have never left."

Sal wasn't ready to go that far.

"Where were you?" Gemma asked.

Sal shook his head and hunched his shoulders. "Wherever," he said. Which was what he said almost every time he stayed out all night and Gemma asked him that question. It was as if he was determined to keep some control over his existence that she had no power over.

But all his flippant answer did was to piss Gemma off all over again. And she moved completely out of his embrace and headed for the exit.

"Gem, wait," said Sal as he turned and grabbed her arm again.

"I'm late for court," she said, removed her arm from his grasp, and left.

Sal was about to hurry out of that door

after her. But he heard his son's voice. "She's late, Dad," he said. "Let her go."

Sal turned around and saw Lucky standing at the far end of the foyer holding the baby. Then Lucky walked up to his father and handed the baby to him. "I've got to get ready for school," he said, and headed back toward his bedroom.

Teresa opened her big bright eyes as soon as she smelled her father's scent. Then she smiled a big smile that Sal needed. And he smiled right back at her. If Gemma had his heart, he had a feeling that one day Teresa would have his soul. That was how much he loved his baby girl. And he pulled her into his arms even tighter.

But he couldn't stop thinking about his wife.

CHAPTER SEVEN

Is there somebody else?

That was the question Sal Gabrini couldn't shake as he buttoned his double-breasted suitcoat and walked down the air steps of his private jet. Four days had passed since they had that blowup at the cookout. That next day, after Gemma left for work, he had to suddenly leave town for a few days to handle some syndicate shit in Chicago that required his level of attention. He had just arrived back in town. He had phoned and told Gemma he would be back that afternoon and he had hoped she would be at the airfield to greet him. She didn't seem angry with him for suddenly leaving town since she knew he was the head of the Gabrini Crime Family and it be that way sometimes. At least he didn't hear it in her voice when he phoned her. But you could never tell with Gemma. The fact that she didn't show up at the airport to greet him proved that.

The only person he saw standing beside the SUV waiting to greet him was Robby Yale, his underboss. And even Robby didn't look thrilled to see his ass either. Sal could feel the animosity from across the tarmac. Another source of contention Sal couldn't understand because Robby wasn't a talker either. He wasn't explaining his problems either. It was like how many ways could one man fuck up without anybody bothering to tell him why? Sal was getting tired of being everybody's punching bag. He was getting tired of this shit.

"Howya Robby?" Sal said as he approached his SUV.

"Hey Boss," Robby grunted, not in his usual upbeat voice, but in a dry monotone as he opened the back passenger door for Sal. "How did it go?"

"Problem averted for now," Sal said as

he got into the SUV. But when Robby seemed to slam the door shut and then hop in on the front passenger seat as if it was a bother for him to even be there, Sal had had enough. "What the fuck is your problem, Robby?"

Robby turned around and looked at the boss as if he was utterly confused. "Who said I got a problem? I ain't got no problem."

"Next time you slam my door I'll slam your fucking head against that dashboard. Then you'll have a problem. You feel me?"

Sal could tell Robby didn't want to respond, but he knew Sal never issued idle threats. "Yes, sir."

"Where's my wife?"

"Last I spoke to Pauley he said she had a long day in court and then went straight to her office."

"Did she eat anything at the courthouse?"

"He didn't want to blow his cover so he wasn't following her that closely. He figured she was safe in the courthouse," Robby added, as his phone began ringing.

Sal exhaled. Gemma was naturally slender, but he could tell, last time he held her, that she was losing a little weight. Which meant she wasn't taking care of herself right. Which only underscored his original concern: something was going on with Gemma! "Take me to her office," he said to Fast Eddie, his driver, as Robby answered his phone.

But when Robby ended the call, he turned toward Sal with urgency in his voice. "We got trouble, Boss."

"What trouble?"

"They took out Brick's outfit."

"Motherfuckers!"

"The only one still breathing is the son."

Sal was shocked. "What do you mean the only one? *Everybody's gone*?"

"Everybody."

Sal could hardly believe it. "Where's the boy?"

"At Carla's place. He's got about five slugs in him, though, Boss. But he's still breathing."

"Get me there fast," Sal ordered Eddie, and Fast Eddie sped away.

Sal leaned back in his seat. The last thing he needed was a war. But Brick was under the Gabrini Syndicate. Brick was one of the smaller outfits that relied on Sal's protection and, in exchange, was loyal and did whatever small jobs Sal needed done. If somebody went after Brick's outfit, they knew Sal would get involved.

"What the fuck is wrong with these people?" asked an infuriated Robby. "Who in their right mind would pull you into this turf war bullshit? Who in their right mind would start a war they know they can't win?"

Sal didn't know the answer to those questions either. All he knew was that Joe Brusconi, who they called Brick, was dead, and so was his entire outfit with the exception of his son. If that didn't signify balls, *or lunacy*, Sal didn't know what did.

That was why, when they arrived at Carla's, a small jazz club in west Las Vegas, there was no hesitation. Sal and Robby hopped out and hurried to the club's front entrance. It was late afternoon and the club didn't open until nightfall, but the bouncer was waiting and opened the door for Sal and his powerful underboss.

Carla, the tall black owner and a longtime friend of Sal's, was seated at the bar with her club's manager, and she nodded toward the back. Sal knew she didn't like dealing with that mob shit for fear of losing her liquor license, but he also knew she wouldn't have a liquor license if it wasn't for him. She was reliable when they needed a hideout.

When they made it to the backroom and opened the door, Luke Brusconi, Brick's kid, was lying on a sofa being attended to by Hands, an ex-con who was stripped of his right to practice medicine decades ago. He was wrapping the kid in large fabric bandages, but that was only to staunch the bleeding.

"We gotta get him to a hospital," was the first thing Hands said when Sal and Robby walked in. "There's no way around it."

"Then call an ambulance," said Robby.

"Oh hell no you ain't calling no ambulance here," said Carla. Everybody turned around. She had followed Sal and Robby to the back and was standing at the door. "I'm opening soon. You get him away from here and call your ambulance wherever you take him."

"Who bought him here?" asked Sal.

"Some Italian that looks like all you Italians. He pushed him out of a car at my doorstep and kept on going. When I saw who it was, I called Hands. Then I called Robby."

"He's in no position to be moved," said Sal. "And we ain't involving no ambulances. You're a surgeon," he added, to Hands. "You'll have to operate on him here."

"That's impossible! My license to practice was suspended twenty years ago."

Robby put a gun to Hands' head. "Come again?"

Hands dropped his head. His life was so off course that there was no way back straight to save his life. "If he dies, it's on your head not mine," said Hands as he grabbed his medical bag.

Sal knelt down beside Luke. He was filled with sweat, and had terror in his eyes. "Who did it, kid?" Sal asked him.

"Hey Boss."

Sal's heart went out to the young guy. He knew for a fact old man Brick never intended for Luke to follow in his footsteps, but Luke wouldn't be denied. Couldn't tell his ass a thing. He didn't want to be anything else but a gangster just like his father. Now look at him. "Hey, son."

"They killed Pop, Mr. G. They killed

everybody. Then they dropped me in front of Miss Carla's place."

"Who's they?"

"I don't know. We never saw it coming. Only face I saw was the driver, who pushed me out of the car and took off."

"Did you recognize him?"

"Never saw him before in my life." Then Luke clutched Sal's arm. "Am I gonna die, Mr. G?"

The terror in that young man's eyes gripped Sal. But he wasn't going to lie to him. "It don't look good, Luke. But you're young and strong."

"I can pull through, can't I, Mr. G?"

Sal smiled at him as the young man clutched him tighter. "Did your old man have any beef with anybody? I know he had those turf issues with Snide. Could Snide's outfit be behind this?"

But Luke was shaking his head. "He's the one that warned us."

This interested Robby too. "Warned you about what?"

"An imminent attack. He said some new guy wants to take over."

"Did he say anything about this guy?"

"Said he wasn't from around here. Said he was from out East. Maybe Jersey. Tried to do the same thing to Monk Paletti's outfit. But the Monk beat him back. Now he's looking for fresher meat."

"Did he know Brick was affiliated with me?"

"Don't know. I was in another room, but I heard Pop about to tell the guy that he was a part of your syndicate, but he didn't get your name out before they took him out. Then I was shot up and went unconscious. I didn't remember anything else until I was in that car with that guy. I can pull through, can't I, Mr. G?"

"Sure you can, kid," said Sal, even as Luke's eyes began to slowly lose their light.

"Sure you can."

And then just like that Luke was gone.

Sal dropped his head. He hated this shit! Then he stood up. "Call a clean up crew, Robby. You stay with the kid, Hands, until they get here."

"Sure thing, Sal."

Then Sal looked at Luke again. "For nothing," he said. "Poor kid."

"Can you believe it?" said Robby. "I'll bet you any amount of money those yahoos didn't know he was affiliated with you. They took out an entire outfit without knowing the facts." Robby shook his head. "Boy are they in for a surprise."

"Don't be so sure," said Sal. "The kid just said they went after Monk Paletti. Monk has the third largest outfit in the country and they went after him. Don't be so quick with the conclusions," Sal warned.

"If they did know about the affiliation," Robby said with a smile, "then they're just plain stupid."

Hands laughed. But for Sal, seeing another one of his people iced, and to know Brick's entire outfit bit the dust too, was nothing to laugh about. Because he had to do something about it. Which meant a war could be brewing. Which meant he had to fight a ghost until he found out who those fuckers were. And he never liked fighting a ghost. That never turned out well.

But when Robby called in the cleanup crew and he and Sal made it back into the SUV, Gemma was back on Sal's mind. "Take me to my wife's office," he ordered Eddie.

CHAPTER EIGHT

Gemma Jones-Gabrini sat on the edge of the bed barely able to move. It was hump day, but she didn't get over that hump. She came home early from work and went straight to bed. Was just that exhausted.

What's wrong with me?

She'd been in a funk for months now when she knew she should have been happy. She was going out for drinks later that evening with three of her sorority sisters whose flight was on a three-hour layover. They phoned that morning and asked if she could take a little time out of her busy schedule and meet them at a bar near the airport for drinks, and to catch up on old times. It was her pleasure, were they kidding? She hadn't seen Bev, Laura, nor Jasmine in years! But they always looked up to Gemma, and they knew she was now one of the most sought-after criminal defense attorneys in the country.   They said it would be their honor if she could meet with them, as if they just knew she was still that special lady. She could barely get out of bed. She was *special* alright.

She made her way into the ensuite bathroom and peed like Sal usually did: long and drawn out. As if it would never end. But when it finally did and she stood at the marbled vanity washing her hands and staring at herself in the mirror, she suddenly felt as if something was missing. And that was when it hit her. Her baby. *Where was her baby*?

She ran back into the bedroom and grabbed her iPhone off of the nightstand. When she pulled up the house security monitors, she saw her beautiful baby girl fast asleep, her big green eyes and dark-brown skin at peace with the world as she slept on her teenage brother's chest. Lucky was on his phone talking, Gemma was sure, to one of his little girlfriends. But she smiled and relaxed. Despite what Carmine said his nickname implied, Lucky was a young man you could rely on. Everybody at his private prep school certainly did. He was president of the student body, captain of the baseball team, co-captain and quarterback of the football team, and vice-president of the honor society. He would have been president of that organization too, Gemma was convinced, but his cousin Carmine was the unanimous choice for Honor Society President. So Teresa, her daughter, was in good hands and just fine.

But why wasn't Gemma feeling fine herself? And it wasn't post-partum depression, she didn't care how many times Sal told her that. Tee was eight months old. And although she read somewhere that PPD could happen as late as eighteen months after birth, she wasn't buying it. She was just working too hard, was the best she could come up with.

But just as she put down her phone to

make her way to the shower, it rang. When she saw on the Caller ID that it was Curtis, her secretary, she answered quickly. "I know I told you I might come back to the office today, but I'm not coming back in. I overslept."

"No worries," said Curtis. "I was getting ready to leave myself. I just wanted to let you know Judge Dawkins called."

Terror suddenly gripped Gemma. "Don't tell me he's reconvening?"

"No, no, it's not court-related. At least I don't think so. He wanted to know if you could meet him for a drink tonight."

That surprised Gemma. She respected Rory Hawkins. Viewed him as one of her mentors early in her career. But they never socialized outside of court. "Why would he want to meet with me?"

"That was precisely what your husband said when he was here earlier."

Did Gemma hear him right. "Sal was at the office?"

"Robby dropped by to wish me happy birthday and Mr. Gabrini was with him. He assumed you would be here too. I told him you went home early. But that didn't stop him from listening to my entire phone conversation like it was his right to listen since it involved you. And you could tell he didn't like for a second the idea of his woman having drinks with some man, especially a ladies man like Judge Dawkins."

"But did you ask the judge why he wanted to have drinks with me? I have cases pending before his court. On its face it's highly inappropriate."

"I know!" Curtis always spoke in exclamation. He could be the biggest drama king alive. "And yes I did ask him why. All he said was that he wanted to discuss a personal matter with you."

"A personal *legal* matter?" Gemma was a highly-regarded criminal defense attorney in Vegas. And among her firm's expansive client list were judges too. "It has to be a personal legal matter."

"That's what I'm assuming too," Curtis said. "But I don't know that to be fact."

"Well what did you tell him?"

"I told him you already had plans to meet with friends at Gateshead bar tonight."

Gemma shook her head. It was a bit too much information to just be giving out in her view, but trying to tame Curtis's diarrhea mouth was like trying to tame Tee's crying. If she felt like crying, she was going to cry - and ears be damned. If Curtis felt like talking, he was going to talk - and privacy be damned. It was one of his greatest weaknesses. But he had so many strengths that there was no way Gemma was getting rid of him. Although she would talk to him about that mouth of his later. "What did he say when you told him that?"

"Nothing. Just hung up. You know how he is. But Mr. Gabrini had a lot to say."

"Such as?"

"Who were these friends you were having drinks with. Stuff like that."

Gemma crossed her legs and closed her eyes. She hadn't planned on telling Sal about going out for drinks because she knew he'd give her his usual *who, what, when, why* third-degree questions and she just wasn't in the mood to hear all that. She knew it was for her protection: she understood he was always worried about her and the kids. But lately it was beginning to feel suffocating. "Okay, Curtis, I'll see you tomorrow."

"Have fun tonight! Cha-cha," Curtis said, and ended the call.

Gemma opened her eyes, and then sat her phone back down. She wanted to just go back to bed and sleep until next week. But she knew that wasn't possible. She got up and headed for the shower. She knew she had to meet her friends. No matter how she felt, she wasn't letting her girls down.

But she couldn't shake the feeling that it

was going to be a long night tonight.

CHAPTER NINE

Sal parked his Bugatti in the alleyway of Gateshead bar and stepped out just as the side door of the bar was opened for him. He buttoned his double-breasted Armani suit and made his way inside. It was ten at night. Sal already had so much on his plate it was ridiculous. But no way was he going to hear that his wife was meeting some old college friends she never bothered to mention, and he just let it slide. It could be a set up. According to Curtis, Gem hadn't seen these girls in years. And suddenly out of the blue they wanted to meet, and meet at some hideaway bar near the airport? Sal was super-busy with his syndicate and his legit businesses, but he was checking this out.

He made his way down a narrow hallway that led, not into the belly of the bar, but into the owner's office. The owner, Clyde Cappanelli, was seated behind his desk when Sal walked in.

"Ever hear of knocking? You should try it sometime."

"Ever hear of shutting your trap? You should try it sometime."

Clyde grinned, stood to his feet, and extended his hand. "How you doing Sal Luca?" They shook hands. "I haven't seen your gangster ass in a month of Sundays."

"Maybe that should tell you something."

Clyde laughed at that too.

"They here yet?"

"I can only guess it's them. Three good-looking black ladies, all nicely dressed like professional people. I assume they're here to see your wife. They're the only blacks in here at the moment."

Sal found him presumptive. "Who said they had to be black? Did I say they had to be black?"

"You said they were her sorority sisters. Most sororities are segregated, Sal, even in this day and age. Believe it or not."

"What would you know about anything related to college?"

"I got a kid that goes to one. I'm learning stuff."

"Just show them to me," Sal said as he walked around the desk where Clyde's monitors were located.

Clyde sat back down and pulled up the cameras that covered the front interior of his bar. Then he zoomed in on a table where three black ladies were seated. "That's them," he said. "Look like they fit the bill to me."

But Sal wasn't ready to conclude anything as he watched the ladies sip from their drinks and laugh and talk. If Gemma was a part of that group, she hadn't arrived yet.

"Wanna hear their conversation?" asked Clyde.

Sal looked at him. "You can hear the

conversations?"

"Absolutely. I wanna hear everything that goes on in my bar. But I don't use any of it against anybody."

"Bullshit."

"Do you wanna hear what their talking about or not?"

Sal gave the nod and Clyde turned on the volume. All three ladies were distinctive in Sal's eyes: the tallest, the shortest, and the cutest.

"Not even close," said the shortest.

"I know," said the cutest. "But what can we do? We've got to hope she's willing."

"And if she's not?" asked the tallest.

"That's not an option. She has to be willing."

"Wonder what that's about?" Sal said as he and Clyde continued watching and listening.

"Think they talking about your old lady?"

"How should I know? I don't know these dames from a hole in the wall. How should I know who they're talking about?"

But then the cutest asked, "is that her?" And then they all looked out of the window too.

Although Clyde's interior cameras couldn't capture Gemma's arrival outside because he would have to change screens altogether, the ladies had plenty to say about it.

"She looks exactly the same," said the tallest.

"I wouldn't say exactly the same," said the shortest. "We haven't seen her in years. But close enough."

"She's had a baby eight months ago and still managed to keep that same fine figure she had in college," said the cutest. "I don't care what you say. You gotta give her that."

"Yeah, but she's still black," the shortest said to them, and they all looked at her.

"We're all black," said the cutest. "What's that supposed to mean, Bev?"

"She's very dark-skinned. That's all I'm saying."

"We're all dark-skinned," said the tallest. "Including you, Bev. You're just a lighter shade of dark than the rest of us. So what?"

"So nothing. I'm a lot lighter than the rest of you, but that's no biggie."

"It sure damn ain't," said the cutest.

"You need to quit, Bev," said the tallest.

Then the shortest smiled. "I was just joking around. Dang girls! Can't you take a joke? Besides, what y'all need to be worrying about isn't my little jokes, but that husband of hers."

Clyde grinned "Uh-oh."

But Sal continued staring at them, as if he was taking the measure of what each and every one of them was truly about. And the short one? The one called Bev? He already didn't like.

"Her husband is her business," said the tallest. "We already agreed we will not bring him up if she doesn't. You know Gemma has always guarded her privacy."

"But those articles say he's a reputed mob boss. Not just *in* the mob, which would be bad enough. They say he's the boss of the mob."

"I don't buy it," said the cutest. "Gemma's a lawyer. They would disbar her if she was married to a mob boss. That don't make no kind of sense to me."

"Me either," said the tallest. "But let's not go there. That's not why we're here. We got to focus on having fun. Bump her husband."

"Hey Gemma!" the shortest said with a grand smile as she stood up first to greet the new arrival.

Sal's heart squeezed when Gemma entered the frame. Although one of his capos, Pauley Cobane, was already in the bar to keep an eye on Gemma, Sal always felt overly-protective of her, as if there was a fragility to her that nobody saw or would believe existed. But he saw it daily, and he knew it existed.

She was fragile. She could take people's bullshit all day long, and she did take it, but it stayed with her and bothered her long term. So seeing her standing there in her all white pantsuit with red heels and a red scarf around her neck made him tighten up. He knew he was going to have a hard time containing himself if they didn't treat her right. That little comment about her skin tone already put the short one in his crosshairs. She'd better not come with that bullshit around Gemma, that was all he had to say. She'd better treat her right. Because Gemma was his heart. Nobody was mistreating her.

But even Gemma didn't know she was being followed. But since word came down about Brick's outfit earlier that day, Sal ordered a security detail to follow her wherever she went.

Although Clyde was watching Sal's wife too, he wasn't as impressed as Sal was. To him, the wife of Sal Gabrini should be drop-dead gorgeous, the most beautiful woman in the world kind of girl. Not that his old lady wasn't a pretty lady. She was a very pretty lady. But he wouldn't put her in the drop-dead gorgeous category like he would put the three ladies she was meeting up with. To Clyde, those ladies were supermodel gorgeous. Gemma was just pretty. But Sal loved her to death. There was no doubt in his mind about that!

All three ladies were standing by the time Gemma made it to their table. Gemma did a little shimmy-shimmy dance as she grinned and walked up to them and they all were yelling in excitement after so many years of not seeing her. Pauley stayed back and took a seat at the table directly across from them. It was his job to be there, but not there. Seen, but not noticed.

Gemma's friends certainly didn't notice him. They were too happy to see their longtime friend. And she did not disappoint.

She hugged each of them affectionately. And she put a name to each one of them.

"Hey, Jasmine," she said to the cutest one.

"It's so good to see you, girl," said Jasmine as they hugged. "It's been a long time."

"And look at you Miss Laura," Gemma said to the tallest one as they embraced warmly too. When they stopped embracing, Gemma looked her up and down. "Girl, what's your secret? You haven't aged a day."

"Me? You're the one. And that figure? Honey bye. You're the one who looks great."

"Hey Bev," Gemma said as she embraced the shortest one last, although she was the first one on her feet greeting her. Not that Gemma didn't like the shortest one. She loved the little thing. But even in college, they always had their issues.

"Sit down, sit down," said Laura. "We're so happy you could come by. I know it's out in the boonies and you're busy as a you-know-what."

"No problem at all," said Gemma as they all sat at the table. "I could use a break anyway."

"Life is hard?"

"Tell me about it."

"We ordered a Sherry for you," said Bev. "If that's still your drink."

"Don't you dare," Sal said out loud as he stood, arms folded, in Clyde's office. "That bitch could have dropped a roofie in that drink."

But Gemma wasn't about to put her lips to anything sitting around a table waiting for her. She knew the girls back when, and they were righteous ladies, but that was a long time ago. She called for the waiter to bring her a glass of wine.

Sal nodded. Pleased with his wife. "That's what I'm talking about," he said.

Then an African-American male, very tall and slender, walked up to their table.

Pauley Cobane was ready to stand up and rush over there if need be.

"I know your guy," said Clyde, "but who's the other guy?"

Sal said nothing. He had no idea either.

"Mrs. Gabrini?"

Gemma looked up and saw that Judge Hawkins was standing at her table. But what she didn't see was that Sal's capo was about to make his move too, should the guy do more than just talk. Gemma smiled when she recognized who it was. "Hello Judge Hawkins. What are you doing here?"

"Did your secretary tell you that I had phoned?"

"Yes, sir, he told me you called the office."

"Why didn't you phone me back?"

Gemma found his question unnecessary, but he was a man she'd always respected for his tireless work on behalf of the poor and disenfranchised. She wasn't trying to diss him. "It was my intent to phone you back tomorrow when I returned to my office."

"When I'm the one phoning, you don't wait until tomorrow. You phone me back immediately. Are we clear?"

Sal and Clyde both were surprised by the man's tone. "Well damn," said Clyde. "You gonna let that suit talk to your old lady like that, Sal?"

But Sal didn't say a word. He was watching the guy's every move. If he posed any physical threat to his wife, Pauley would be able to handle him until Sal could get out there.

"Are we clear, Gemma?" the judge asked her again.

But Gemma didn't care how many times he asked her. She wasn't responding to anybody who spoke to her that way. Judge or no judge.

And it worked. The judge moved on. "I came out here because it couldn't wait."

He was talking as if they had had a prior

conversation about some matter, when they had not. "What couldn't wait?"

"My vocalizing my displeasure with your conduct, young lady. That's what!"

Gemma was lost. So were her friends. "Sir, what are you talking about?"

"The Frazier case."

"What about the Frazier case?"

"That young man is on his way to Death Row because of your incompetence!"

Gemma was offended, but not defensive. She stared at him.

"You're the worst lawyer that has ever stepped foot in my courtroom!"

Her friends were shocked. So was Sal. He unfolded his arms and stared unblinkingly at the arrogant judge.

But Hawkins was undeterred by the looks of shock around him. "You were unprepared, didn't ask any questions, and didn't even put your client on the stand to fight for his life."

"That was my client's decision and you know it," Gemma shot back.

"Any other attorney would have made him get on that stand."

"He had a record as long as this building. The prosecution would have destroyed him. And besides, I couldn't force him to take the stand and you know it. That would be unethical."

"Unethical?" Hawkins now seemed offended. "What would you know about ethics?"

Clyde was shocked that ANYBODY would talk to Sal Gabrini's wife that way. Her friends were shocked that anybody would talk that way to the Gemma Jones they remembered too.

But it didn't matter to Hawkins. He kept right on talking. "Ethics would not be the word you should ever find on your lips, are you kidding me? You're married to a mobster for crying out loud. A Mafia man. A thug. Don't you dare talk to me about ethics!"

Gemma had had enough. "You need to leave, Judge."

"You don't tell me what to do."

Gemma stood up. Sal's man stood up too, but kept his distance. "I'm telling you to give me some feet. I'm telling you to get your ass up out of my face."

Her friends smiled. Gemma was never ghetto, but she was never a pushover either. And to talk to a judge that way! A man she had to appear before? They were impressed.

But Gemma wasn't thinking about impressing anyone. She was just pissed that this man could come at her like she was his doormat.

And he kept on coming. "I have notified the Bar of your reckless incompetence, and I am personally asking the appeals court to grant Frazier a new trial on the basis of your incompetent defense alone. You're a disgrace to the legal profession and the sooner you're disbarred and not allowed to defend anybody else can't come soon enough for me. The blood of that young man is on your hands, Gemma Jones. You worthless pile of shit. I hope you rot in hell for what you did!" And then Hawkins turned and began leaving the bar.

But Sal was already hurrying toward the exit, to get his hands on that bastard before he left the scene. Nobody talked to his wife that way. Nobody!

But Clyde saw something else. "Wait, Sal," he said.

Sal glanced back, but he kept hurrying toward the door.

"He's not alone. He's got a cop escort."

Sal stopped in his tracks. "A cop?" He hurried back over to Clyde's desk and saw a uniformed policeman waiting for the judge at the entrance doors. And then they walked outside.

Clyde left the interior camera screens, and pulled up the monitors for the exterior cameras. And that was when they saw the cop open the car door for the judge, the judge got in, and then the cop got behind the wheel and drove him away.

"Why would a cop be escorting a judge around?" asked Sal.

"Probably got some death threats," said Clyde, "and the judge needed protection."

It wasn't Sal's style, but he now knew he would have to handle Hawkins the *Backdoor Tommy* way: later. Besides, Gemma would be royally pissed if he blew his cover and revealed that he was checking on her. "Pull back up the interior cameras," he said. He wanted to make sure she was okay.

Gemma was thrown so off guard that she was stupefied. She was so not expecting to be berated by a judge she'd always respected, and she didn't know what to do. Or what to say. Or how to react!

"What was that all about?" asked Bev as she leaned toward Gemma.

127

"Was the young man you defended some kin to him?" Laura asked.

"He couldn't be," said Jasmine, "if he was the presiding judge."

But Gemma didn't answer any of their questions. Because she didn't know any of the answers. Because she was still reeling by the massive brow-beating she'd just taken.

But Gemma was a consummate pro. She knew how to keep it moving. "Somebody didn't have their Xanax today," she joked, the ladies laughed, and they moved on too.

They finished their drinks and talked happily about the good old days as if that Hawkins episode never happened. And they explained the real reason why they wanted to meet with Gemma: They wanted her to be the keynote speaker at their upcoming sorority event. But Sal could see she was still reeling from what happened with Hawkins. He could see the hurt all over her face. She was devastated. Which meant he was too.

He walked away from Clyde and put a call into Robby Yale, his underboss, ordering him to get certain intel on that judge. And then he walked back over to the monitors. Gemma was still smiling, and still moving on, but she wasn't pulling it off. The ladies seemed to believe she was, and Clyde seemed to believe so too. He even said so. But Sal knew better.

CHAPTER TEN

With one hard, long thrust he was so deep inside of her that she had to arch her back to receive all of him. Which she gladly did. They were at home, in bed, and neither knew that they both had been at that same bar when Hawkins showed his ass. Sal was waiting for word on where that bastard was. He could hardly wait to pay a visit to that asshole. But right now he had a woman to satisfy. Gemma never mentioned it. Lately, she never mentioned much of anything to Sal. But he knew she was hurt.

That was why he was determined to leave it all inside of her. His first move always dictated the urgency, or desperation, or need that always turned their lovemaking into something so much more than just making love. He got in as deep as he could and as aggressively as he could to give her an immediate jolt. And then he began moving slowly inside of Gemma. Slow and steady. The way he knew she liked it.

And Gemma needed it that night. After what happened at Gateshead bar, she was still disturbed. Her *soro* sisters thought the reason the rest of their get together had that edge of tension around it was because Judge Hawkins had embarrassed her in front of them. But Gemma didn't give a shit about what it looked like. It was what he said to her that cut her to her core. It was when he said Joel Frazier was on Death Row because of her incompetence at trial, which she knew wasn't true. She gave her all to that loser of a case. That boy was guilty every which way from Sunday and Hawkins knew it. The jury knew it, too, and that was why he was on Death Row. But Hawkins came at her as if it was all her fault. A judge she respected so completely, and had in

131

some ways considered him a mentor for his sound advice through the years, now hated her? Where did that come from?

But even thoughts of that judge could not dampen how Sal was doing her. Because he was on top of her pumping his ass off and she was feeling the wonderment of his hard work. Her arms and legs were wrapped around him and her hands couldn't stop racing through his hair as he moved his dick inside of her in his special way. A way where every movement was hitting her right where she needed it to hit. She was moaning and groaning and feeling every single move he made.

Sal knew she was enjoying it as much as he was too. And not just by the guttural sounds she was making, but mainly by the way her beautiful eyes were so hooded with love and lust that he pumped on her even harder to make sure she kept that look. And she kept it. Every time he leaned up to see it for himself, she had that look he loved. And he pumped even harder.

They made love for nearly an hour. It was how Sal rolled and Gemma loved that about him. He wasn't a young man anymore. He couldn't hang the way he used to hang when they first got together. Back then, nobody would mistake Sal for some two-minute man. He was more like a two-hour man! But even now he was still hanging in there far better than anybody Gemma had ever been with in her entire life. He was still her gold standard.

And when he took them all the way over that cliff, they both came within seconds of each other. They came with a thunderous cum.

Then Sal, his body sweat-filled and drained as if he had poured all of himself into Gemma, collapsed on top of her.

Gemma felt his dead weight, but she was still feeling his penis inside of her. She was still in the throes of her exceptionally intense orgasm. Sal had put it on her that night. He had taken her there. Getting back from that state of euphoria was hard.

And when he pulled out of her, she immediately felt empty again.

He rolled off of her and laid on his back. She remained on her back as both of them were still coming down from that mountain Sal's dick had put them on. But after several minutes, he was back to normal enough to pull her into his arms. Then he wrapped both arms around her. And he looked at her. "You okay?"

Gemma managed to smile. "Very much so."

"Anything you want to talk to me about?"

Gemma knew she should have told Sal about how Hawkins treated her at Gateshead bar, but she couldn't pull herself to do it. Sal wouldn't take it lying down. He would declare he could, but she knew he wouldn't. She wasn't putting him in that position. "No," she said. "All's good."

Sal exhaled. Gemma never was a talkative person. She never told him everything going on with her and he knew it. But damn. The way that judge spoke to her needed to be addressed, and Gemma should know that.

"Babe, what's wrong?"

"Nothing's wrong, Sal."

"Yes, it is. You've been a shell of yourself lately. And tonight you seemed even worse."

"Worse? I didn't hear you requesting any refunds, honey."

Sal looked at her. "You know I'm not talking about that. I'm talking about you. Something's wrong, Gem. I know you."

"I said I'm okay."

"You're not okay! Let's at least agree to that very real fact that you're not okay. And I'm not taking this shit anymore. You're going to

135

counseling to get this figured out."

"Counseling?" Gemma shook her head. "I'm not talking to some stranger about my business."

"Then you're talking to Tony." Tony Sinatra was a clinical psychologist in the family and Big Daddy Sinatra's second-oldest son. He was everybody's go-to for their mental health.

When Gemma didn't object to Tony, Sal felt a sense of relief. Finally she was agreeing to something! "I'll call him in the morning," he said.

Gemma said nothing. She cuddled even closer against Sal and let time, and his big, protective arms, put her to sleep.

Before day that next morning, Sal eased out of bed and went to one of their numerous guest rooms to brush, shower, and dress without disturbing Gemma. Before he could make it downstairs, his phone vibrated. It was

Robby Yale.

"What you got?"

"The cop guarding his place just left. Perfect time to make our move," Robby said.

CHAPTER ELEVEN

Sal drove his Bugatti into the parking garage of the condominium building with Robby on the passenger seat. When he found an empty visitor parking spot, he took it.

But Robby looked at him. "Boss, can I ask you something?"

Sal shifted his gear to Park. "What?"

"You good? You and Mrs. G, I mean?"

Sal hesitated. "Not necessarily. Why?"

"Curtis says she's been acting different at work lately."

"Different how?"

"Different. Not the same old person. He says it's like she's got the weight of the world on her shoulders."

Sal ran his hand across his face. "I don't know what's going on. She won't talk to nobody. Not even Reno's old lady, who she always used to confide in. And now this asshole shows up, as if she needed to hear his bullshit."

"I know you didn't need to hear it either. Not after what happened with Brick's outfit. Another thing you got to deal with. Because we gotta deal with it, Boss. No way they can wipe out our affiliate and we do nothing about it."

"I need to talk to Monk Paletti. Luke said they tried to muscle in on Monk before they came for Brick."

"As if Monk Paletti was gonna let anybody muscle him out of anything," Robby said.

"But first things first," said Sal as he began unbuckling his seatbelt.

Robby looked at him. "She's always first, isn't she?"

"Damn right."

"You really love her, Boss. Don't you?"

Sal hesitated. He didn't go that deep

with anybody but Gemma. "Yes," he said.

"I know what that's like now," said Robby.

Sal and Robby exchanged a glance. Robby and Curtis were still together, but nobody in the mob world fully accepted it. They all tolerated it because Sal laid down the law: Robby was his underboss, he told them, and they had better recognize. Robby would forever love Sal for having his back like that. But that didn't mean old school Sal was down for whatever. He wasn't exactly Robby and Curtis's cheerleader. It was more like *don't ask, don't tell* with Sal.

"Let's go handle some business," Sal said, and got out of the car.

CHAPTER TWELVE

Rory Hawkins stood at the window of his high-rise condo sipping his wine and talking to himself in mumbles only he could understand. How did it all get so off track? How did he let it happen? He was so tired of this shit he didn't know what to do. But he had to hold on. He had to keep showing up like he hadn't a care in this world and hold on. Tonight was the turning point. He hated dragging Gem into it, but he had no choice. She could take it. He knew it when he first met her and would give her advice about her career and would treat her like she was his prodigy.

But that outcome was unforgiveable. He gave her every break during that trial.

Every motion was in her favor. Everything she presented, he allowed in. He made it clear to the jury that he was on her side. And she still couldn't bring it home. He still ended up on Death Row. She let him down. He thought she knew how to play dirty too.

But fuck it, he decided as he made his way into his kitchen and poured the last of his wine down the sink. He'd deal with that shit another day. Right now, he was going to bed.

He walked down the hall that led to his master bedroom. But as soon as he crossed the threshold, he was shocked when a younger man grabbed him by his shirt and threw him across his bedroom, slamming his body against the wall.

"Who are you?" he cried out in agony. He'd never seen the guy before. "How did you get in my home? Who are you?"

But Robby didn't give a fuck about whether he knew him or not. Sal had told Robby what went down at that bar. Robby, who loved Gemma, wanted a piece of that asshole too. "Think you got the balls to mess with the man's wife?" Robby violently squeezed Hawkins' balls, causing Hawkins to cry out again. "Think you got the balls to fuck with his wife?"

"You're hurting me! Please stop!"

Robby did stop. Not because asshole told him to, but because he could hear the boss walking up the hall. And the boss only told him to secure his ass, not to decimate it.

And then Sal walked into the room.

When Hawkins saw that well-dressed thug walk into his bedroom like he owned the joint, he already knew it was all about his interaction with Gemma earlier that night. But did it take all this? He didn't even lay hands on that bitch. Why did it need the boss himself, and his goon beside, to handle something that amounted to nothing more than a tongue lashing? Hawkins knew he didn't understand the mob in any way, shape or form, but he also sensed that he was about to pay for his miscalculation.

Sal at first walked around the spacious room looking at the junk on the dresser and the two nightstands neatly beside the big bed. Then he took a seat in the chair against the wall by the entrance door. He folded his legs and then nodded to Robby. Robby removed his grip on Hawkins and Hawkins jerked away from him as if he still had the control. But he was no fool. He knew he was by no means out of danger.

"You know who I am," Sal said to Hawkins as if it was a fact.

"Yes, I know who you are. But this person slammed me against this wall and--"

"Who am I?"

Hawkins frowned. What did that have to do with anything at all? "You're Gemma Jones-Gabrini's husband."

"And?"

"And you're a mobster." He wanted to

say thug.

"A mobster," Robby had laughter in his voice. "Get a load of this guy! He's calling you a mobster, Boss."

"What I meant to say is that you are believed to be the head of the Gabrini Crime Family," Hawkins said, correcting himself. "That's what I meant to say."

"You say I'm the head of the Gabrini Crime Family, which sounds pretty dangerous to me," Sal said. "But yet in still you disrespect *my* wife? A guy like me who's supposedly the head of this dangerous, criminal outfit? Are you out of your fucking mind?"

"I don't know what she told you, but I didn't lay a hand on her," Hawkins said defiantly.

"What the fuck difference does that make?" Robby yelled at him. "Didn't you hear the man you moron? You disrespected *his* woman. *His* lady. *His* wife. You disrespected *his*!"

Hawkins understood in that moment the gravity of what he'd done. Gemma wasn't just a thug's wife. She was the wife of the head of a thug organization. One of the most powerful, and by extension most dangerous thug organizations in the world. And her husband, the leader of the gang, was pissed. "I meant no disrespect," said Hawkins. "It was all about a case she worked. It was a professional dress down, and nothing more than that."

Sal was staring at the judge. "What's your game?"

The judge was confused. "Game? What game?"

"You know who I am. You know what happens when anybody goes for my wife. You're a judge, your ass know what you were getting yourself into when you went for her. You already knew. But you did it anyway. Now either you're crazy, or you got something going. Which is it?"

"It's neither. I disagreed with the way

your wife handled a death penalty case and I told her so. That's it. That's all."

"You feel me?"

Hawkins frowned. "I what you?"

"You feel me?"

"No, sir. I do not *feel* you, whatever that means."

Sal continued to stare at him. "You're attracted to my wife?"

Hawkins thought about it. That might be more palatable for both of them than the real reason. "She came on to me initially," he said, "but I rebuked her."

It was another grave miscalculation by a man who was so out of his depth that he was treading water. Because as soon as he confessed his attraction to Gemma, Sal's anger took over and he jumped from that chair and rushed Hawkins. "You lying motherfucker!" Sal yelled as he grabbed him and beat the snot out of him. He threw him around that room like he was as light as a rag doll, and then he knocked him to the floor and began kicking him and stomping him like he was a mangy dog in the street. Hawkins was screaming in pain, but Sal kept on stomping.

Then he got down on Hawkins' level and grabbed Hawkins' hand. "This is a reminder that you keep your ass away from my wife no matter what the cost. And you'd better stop lying on her. I don't want you thinking about her, or ever allowing her name to cross your fucking lips." Then he bent Hawkins hand back until every bone in that hand broke in two. Even Robby cringed. But Hawkins was crying out in unbearable pain as he banged on the floor with his other hand.

"You feel me now?" Sal yelled at him above his cries. "You feel me now, motherfucker?!"

Hawkins was nodding *yes* with the kind of vigor that was almost cartoonish. But he understood who he was dealing with now. He understood his wrong calculations and deadly miscalculations all too clearly now. He would have nodded his head off if he had to.

When Sal was satisfied that his ass got the picture, he stood up, gave him another swift kick, and then looked over at Robby. Then he left the room.

Robby knew what that look meant. Give Hawkins the talk and then meet Sal at Sal's car. Robby didn't like when he had to play clean up. He felt, as the underboss of the second most powerful mob outfit in the world, he was better than this. They should have had some frontline capo to do this simple-ass work. But lately Sal had Robby doing all kinds of jobs beneath his rank. Way beneath it. And Robby was getting tired of it.

But he did as he was told. He walked over to an agonized Hawkins, who was still crying over his broken hand. Hawkins was so terrified that he repelled when Robby knelt down next to him. But Robby just wanted to leave it clean. "Who was just here?" he asked

Hawkins.

"Your boss." When Hawkins realized that was not the right answer, he quickly corrected himself. "I mean, nobody."

"Damn right," said Robby. "Who broke your hand?"

Hawkins was holding the hand in grave agony. "Nobody."

"Who'll break your life if you tell somebody?"

"Nobody."

Robby jumped up and stomped on him.

"I mean," Hawkins said quickly, but he really didn't know what to say.

"I'll say it again," said Robby, "who'll break your life if you tell somebody?"

"Sal Gabrini," Hawkins said quickly, understanding the game now.

"Say that name again?"

"Sal Gabrini."

"*Got*damn right. Now forget that name, you feel me?"

Hawkins was nodding vigorously again. "Yes, sir. I feel you."

"And don't you forget how it felt the next time you even think about disrespecting Mrs. G. Especially if she comes before you in your courtroom." And then Robby hesitated, staring at the arrogant judge, pitying him not a twit, and then he left too.

CHAPTER THIRTEEN

The elevator doors opened and Sal stepped off into the building's parking garage and made his way to his car. His head was pounding. He had been this close to killing that motherfucker. Claiming Gemma came onto him. *Gemma*? Coming onto to *him*? The nerve of that guy! He knew that asshole was lying. If anybody would be pulling shit like that it would be Sal, not Gemma, and Sal knew it.

But he still couldn't bury his head in the sand and act as if nothing was wrong. Something was up. He didn't know what, but he knew Gem had been acting different lately. She never was a chatterbox to begin with, but it was never this bad. Was she getting tired of him? Was she ready to move on? Was she going to break his heart?

He couldn't even think about something

that incredible. If Gemma left him, it would be as if his heart left his body. He couldn't live without her.

His Bugatti unlocked as he approached it, and he was just about to grab the door handle when he felt a two-by-four slam into the back of his legs and take him to his knees. Although shocked, he wasn't so thrown that he couldn't fight back. He was reaching for his gun and fighting to get back on his feet all at once.

But just as he was about to get back up, he felt another blow, this one to the back of his head, and it caused him to fall over. This time he could feel the pain. But he still tried to get back up, to fight those fuckers, but he fell right back down. His gun went in one direction, his phone went in the opposite direction. He heard voices talking, but all he saw was darkness. Then he didn't hear anything at all.

When Sal Gabrini fell, the two men in ski masks that had ambushed him, grabbed him up. The stockier man lifted him by his arms as the muscular man lifted him by the legs. A third man in a similar ski mask grabbed Sal's gun, stole Sal's keys from his pocket, and then hopped into his Bugatti as a cargo van drove up. The stockier man opened the van doors, and then both men tossed Sal inside. The two men then hopped into the van with Sal, and the van and the Bugatti sped away before they could even close the van's door good.

"Shit!" yelled the muscular man as he removed his ski mask and nearly fell out of the van grabbing the flapping door by the handle and then slamming it shut.

The stockier man laughed. "You wouldn't make it on the football field," he said. "That's for damn sure. Too clumsy."

"Fuck you," said the muscular one. The stockier one laughed again as he removed his mask too. He gave Sal an injection that would keep him out for hours. Then he sat down too.

Both men were breathing heavily as

they sat on the bench in the back of that cargo van. They understood the magnitude of what they'd just done. They knew they had just abducted the second most powerful mob boss in the world. They realized they did that shit. But this was work. This was business. This was the assignment.

This was also muscle man's ticket to the top. And he didn't give a fuck anymore. He'd been waiting all his life to hit the big time. He watched everybody else advance except for his ass. He watched lesser men move up that chain ahead of him. He wasn't waiting any longer.

Danny Parva himself offered him the top job as the boss of the Parva Group, but only if he proved his mettle with an assignment nobody else would touch, and that Parva said to his face he wouldn't touch either. But there were no other offers on the table. Nobody else was offering him shit. Everybody else was treating him like a doormat laid down for them to trample on. He touched it alright.

But that didn't mean it was easy. It was a tough-ass assignment. And as he looked down at the Big Sal Gabrini, he could feel just how tough it was going to be. But Parva would make him boss if he completed it. Not a supervising capo. Not an underboss. But boss. The head man in charge. He would run the whole motherfucking outfit. And those were clothes that suited him just fine.

But he had to prove his mettle first. And he was going to prove it. No matter how many bodies he had to crawl over, including Big Sal Gabrini's, he was crawling. He didn't set the rules of engagement: Parva did. He didn't select the target. Parva selected the target. Parva put the deal on the table for anybody with the balls to take it.

He had balls. He was taking that deal.

CHAPTER FOURTEEN

Gemma woke up the next morning surprised that Sal was already gone. The last time she saw him they were in the throes of the kind of passion only Sal was capable of giving to her, and she fully expected to still be in his arms by daybreak, and for him to give it to her again. But he had already gone. Which was a huge letdown. But she knew they hadn't been on the same page for quite some time.

She got out of bed and brushed and showered. By the time she had dressed and made it downstairs, their children were already in the kitchen, having breakfast and doing what they do: debating.

"I'm not saying this team or that team is better. I'm just asking who won?"

"Lebron. Who else?"

"Lebron is not the name of a team. And what do you mean who else? Lebron loses too, Lucky."

"Oh yeah? Like when?"

Marie Gabrini smiled and rolled her eyes. She and her kid brother were at the kitchen table eating breakfast, while their baby sister Teresa was in her highchair making a mess of breakfast. All three of them had the same mother, but Marie had a different father. Her siblings were biracial. She was all black. But Sal had adopted her as his own.

Gemma walked in and headed straight for the baby. Teresa started grinning and flapping her arms as soon as she saw her mother, and Gemma picked her up. "Hey, my little angel. Hey sweetie pie." Then she looked at her older children. "Did your father leave already?"

"Before day this morning, yeah," said Lucky.

"Really?"

"Yup. After you guys did what y'all did and you fell asleep."

Gemma frowned. "How do you know all of that?"

"My room is downstairs. I can't help if Pop has that bed bouncing like he's killing somebody every time y'all do . . . *whatever*."

Marie suppressed a grin.

"Very funny," said Gemma. "Did he tell you where he was going?"

"He didn't tell me anything. I just happened to hear the front door close, So I looked outside. You look good, Ma," Lucky said as he glanced down at Gemma's blue skirt suit and heels. It was a standard lawyer's outfit, but Gemma had a model's body and wore everything well.

"He's right about you looking good," said Marie as she poured their mother a cup of coffee. "But don't be fooled. He's just trying to butter you up, Ma. He wants you to agree with him."

"Agree with him about what?" Gemma bounced the baby in her arms. The baby was trying to grab her earring.

"Lebron James."

"Lebron James? What about Lebron James?"

"Ma," said Lucky, "will you please tell Marie that Lebron is an athletic genius, since she refuses to believe it."

"I didn't say he wasn't a great basketball player. He is a great ball player. After Michael Jordan, he's my number two pick. But what I said is that he's not a team onto himself. He had teammates that helped to make him great."

"Are you kidding me? It's the other way around, Marie! He helps to make *them* great. Like Jordan."

"And that's the big topic of conversation

this morning? Really?" Gemma's phone began to ring. She walked over to her briefcase and reached inside for her phone. "All the problems in this world and that's all you two can debate about?"

"It's Lucky," said Marie. "He always has to be right."

"Not always," said Lucky.

Gemma answered her phone, putting it on Speaker and sitting it on the table because she was holding the baby. "Hey, Robby, what's up?"

"Is Boss there?"

"Here? No. He left before day this morning according to Luck. You haven't heard from him?"

"I was just with him. We had to handle some business. But when I came back out into this parking garage, he was already gone. And all I see is a phone where his car used to be. It looks like his phone."

Gemma's heart dropped. "Oh Lord,"

she said.

Lucky and Marie looked at her. "What's wrong, Ma?" Lucky asked.

"Call your father," Gemma said to him.

Lucky quickly pulled out his phone and called his father. Gemma could hear the phone ringing on Robby's end.

"It's his phone," said Robby, who was holding Sal's ringing phone.

Lucky ended the call. Then he took his mother's phone and put it on Speaker. "What's going on, Robby? My dad okay?"

"Hey, Lucci. We don't know if he is or not."

"Where are you?" asked Gemma as she handed the baby to Marie.

"I'm inside this parking garage. We were handling some business. I'll get one of the guys to pick me up, and then I'll be there."

"I'll call Reno," said Gemma. "He'll know what we should do."

"Just stay there, Robby," Lucky said.

"Uncle Reno will want to come over and see the spot where you found Dad's phone. He'll want you to walk him through Dad's steps before you found his phone."

"That's true."

"Give me the address and I'll head over there too."

"No hell you won't," said Robby. "Your old man's not killing me. Your ass stay right where you are. And that's an order, Lucci."

"Don't worry, he's not going anywhere," said Gemma as she took her phone from Lucky. "Let me call Reno. Reno will call you back, Robby," she added, and then ended the call.

Gemma placed one hand on the side of her now devastated face. "Oh Lord have mercy," she cried out as she attempted to retrieve Reno's phone number. "Have mercy."

"Ma, what's going on?" asked Marie, now looking worried too.

"I don't know." Gemma's face was a

mask of anguish. "We don't know."

Lucky took his mother's phone when she appeared so nervous that she kept pressing the wrong phone number. "I'll call Uncle Reno," he said.

And Marie leaned against her mother. "It'll be alright, Ma," she said as she held baby Teresa. "You just wait and see. Nobody's harming Daddy."

Gemma knew Sal and Marie had a bond. And she appreciated the words of encouragement. But they did little to help. Because Gemma had a feeling. A horrible, sickening feeling. It had been there all morning, but she tried to dismiss it as more of her moodiness lately.

But now she knew better.

Sal always told her to trust her gut. No matter what, go with your gut. Which only made her feel worse because her gut was raging. It was tied all up in knots.

Lucky had to reach out and grab her,

and assist her, as she stumbled to sit down.

CHAPTER FIFTEEN

Reno Gabrini's high-revved Porsche sped into the parking garage of Judge Hawkins' condominium building and drove up to where Robby Yale was waiting. Reno, his suit wrinkled already, as if he had been up all night, and his hair tousled all over the place, hopped out quickly.

Shabby chic was how Robby always described his boss's cousin. Robby hurried over to him. "Hello, sir."

"That's his phone?"

"Yes, sir."

Reno took it from Robby and started typing. Robby was surprised that he knew Sal's password and knew it by heart. But Reno was so anxious and worried that his fingers were unsteady. He had a fixed frown on his face. Because he could feel something wasn't right. No way would Sal just leave his phone, and Robby, like this. No way. His hope was that Sal had initiated the camera when he was approached and there would be some footage. But there was none. Reno also looked at the last call on Sal's phone. It was from Robby before day that morning. "Damn," Reno said.

"Anything, sir?"

"Nothing. We got nothing." Then he looked at Robby. "What about that judge? You think he had something to do with it?"

"I went back up there, to make sure. Sal had already worked him over pretty good. He was too scared to even call an ambulance for himself. He knows what reach we have. And I reminded him of that reach. Besides, he didn't know we were coming, and I literally had just left him when Boss was being snatched. Whoever did it had to have followed us here."

Reno exhaled. Then he looked around. Saw the cameras. "What about the cameras in this joint? You took a look at those?"

"I tried to," said Robby, "but the garage manager wouldn't let me. Said I had to get a court order."

"A court order? And your ass accepted that?"

"Since Boss is missing I didn't want to bring any more heat to the situation. I didn't want cops snooping around."

"I understand that," said Reno, "but fuck that shit. We got to find Sal!"

With Robby following behind him, Reno entered the building and made his way to the ground floor where the garage manager had his booth.

Reno didn't knock. With Robby still behind him, he walked right on in.

The manager, who was seated behind his desk eating hot wings for breakfast, was none too pleased. "I told you I can't just give up film like that. You got to get a court order."

Reno pulled out a gun and pointed it directly at the man's face. "How's this for a court order?"

The manager, surprised, dropped his hot wing and scooted back from his desk.

"Pull up the footage from the fifteenth floor," Reno ordered. "What was the time frame?" he asked Robby.

"It's been about an hour ago."

"For around eight this morning," Reno said.

The manager still just sat there as if it was a movie and not real life. Reno fired that gun within an inch of the manager's head. "You think I'm playing with your ass?" he yelled. "Get that video and get it now!"

"Yes, sir!" The now stunned manager rolled his chair back under his desk and rapidly pulled up the video in question. Reno and Robby went behind the desk and took a closer look. They saw Sal walking to his Bugatti with his phone in his hand. They saw two men in ski masks hiding in front of the car next to Sal's car, and then they jumped him from behind and knocked him down. He pulled out his gun and tried to fight back, but then they knocked him out. They saw Sal's phone and gun drop from his hand. Reno's heart was pounding.

Then they saw another ski-mask-wearing asshole come from out of the frame, grabbed Sal's gun and stole the keys from out of his pocket, and then jumped in his Bugatti as a white van drove up. The two men threw Sal inside, and then the van, and Sal's car, sped off. It was more horrifying than Reno could have imagined. "Get a close up of that license plate," he ordered, and the manager did as he was told.

Robby used his own phone's camera to take a picture of it.

Reno looked at Robby. "Get every single second of footage showing that van's arrival in that garage and when it leaves the garage. I want it all."

"Yes, sir."

"And then read him the riot act," Reno

ordered, and then left.

Robby turned the manager's chair around and placed his hands on the arms of the chair, boxing the manager in. "Let's get a few things clear. You didn't see nothing. You didn't hear nothing. And guess what? You don't know nothing. You understand the language I'm speaking to you?"

The manager was shaking his head. "Yes, sir."

"You don't wanna fuck with us. Trust and believe."

"Yes, sir. I mean no, sir."

"Just so we're clear," Robby said. "Now you heard the man. Get that video."

"Yes, sir," the terrified manager said as he turned to do just that.

But Robby turned his chair back toward him. "And if you try to make a copy of any of that footage, or try any other slick shit, it's not just you we'll come after. It's your wife, your children, and even your mama and your daddy.

So don't be a hero."

"Yes, sir. I mean no, sir," the manager said nervously and did exactly as Reno had instructed.

When Reno walked out of that office, he leaned his already weary body down, his hands on his knees. Sal was in trouble. Serious trouble. Those fuckers were lying in wait for his ass.

He pulled out his phone and made a call to Tommy Gabrini, Sal's older brother and the most levelheaded of the Gabrini men. Reno was tough enough to manage it alone, but he saw that video. This was going to take more than just one heavy-hitter. They needed somebody with the kind of brain power mixed with street smarts that could see what Reno might not be able to see. Tommy was that man.

But when Tommy was told the reason for the phone call, Reno could feel his anguish for his younger brother even over the phone. "We're on our way," Tommy said. Reno didn't even have to tell Tommy to bring his family to avoid any surprise attacks. He always bought his family.

Then Reno phoned his oldest child Jimmy and ordered him to round up the rest of the family in Vegas and get them to Sal and Gemma's house too.

But somebody with the twisted nerve to snatch a man as powerful as Sal Gabrini meant that they believed they were his equal. They believed they had his level of power too. Which made them dangerous as fuck.

That was why Reno also called their uncle Mick Sinatra, the heaviest of heavy hitters. But like usual when trying to reach the man, the call went straight to Voice Mail. But that didn't bother Reno. It was Mick the Tick. You could rarely tell him something he didn't already know.

But as he waited on Robby and thought

about what he saw on that video, he was getting more and more anxious. And fear began to grip him. He was scared for Sal.

He called Mick Sinatra once more.

CHAPTER SIXTEEN

The getaway van roared down the highway as if it was just another cargo van on the job. The driver was the only one up front. The plan was to drive the van well out of Nevada, and far into Utah, before handling their business. Then the kidnappers were to board a private plane and get out of the entire region.

The muscular kidnapper and his stockier partner in crime were in the back of the van, with Sal's still unconscious body lying at their feet.

Dominic "Dommi" Gabrini, Reno Gabrini's son, was the muscular kidnapper.

Archie Jefferson, Gemma Jones-Gabrini's rapist, was his stockier partner in crime.

Archie was looking down at Sal Gabrini

and shaking his head. "When I was younger, me and my baby brother used to ride the bus with our Ma when she went to pick up her paycheck from his wife's office. He would be there sometimes. Wouldn't even speak to me or my brother. With his racist ass."

Dommi frowned. "Racist? How he gonna be racist married to a black woman? Get the fuck out of here! Uncle Sal's no racist."

"Okay he may not be a racist. But he's an asshole." Then Archie shook his head as he continued to stare at Sal. "Even back then we knew he was a gangster. Had Mafia written all over him, I don't care how many double-breasted suits he wore and how many companies he owned. He was a stone-cold gangster to us. And he was the man in our eyes. The biggest of the big men. Even as teenagers we knew he was big. Now look at him. Even big men look small on the floor."

Although Dommi was staring down at his Uncle Sal too, his thought pattern was in a different universe. "It's all Uncle Mick's fault. And Teddy's," he said. "Putting Nikki ahead of me. What kind of bullshit is that? By all rights, when Teddy took over the organization, I should have been decreed underboss. I should have been made number two. But they gave it to Nikki. Just gave it to her!"

"But why is the question," said Archie. "I got no problem with a sister advancing, but even to me that was fast. Why you figure they fucked you around like that?"

"How should I know?"

"Know what I heard?"

Dommi looked at him. "What you heard?"

"I heard Nikki leapfrogged over you and everybody else more qualified in that organization because Teddy was fucking her and Mick wanted to fuck her too. That's what I heard."

Dommi heard that kind of shit too. That Uncle Mick had a thing for Nikki. But that was

too petty a reason. Mick just didn't believe
Dommi could do the job, was the only real
explanation.

But he wasn't about to tell Archie that.

"I don't care what the reason was," he
said, "it was a bad reason. That job was mine
by rights. Why the fuck they think I went to
work for Uncle Mick? For his dental plan? For
his fucking benefits package? I went there to
run the shit."

Archie laughed. "You run Mick Sinatra's
outfit? Yeah, you got balls, Dommi. I'll give
you that. But that man wasn't about to let you
run shit. You killed his son. You killed Joey.
Remember that?"

Best forgotten as far as Dommi was
concerned. He was done explaining that shit a
long time ago.

"But you gotta do what you gotta do,
right? You prove your mettle with this
assignment, then you become underboss
easy."

Dommi nodded. "Yeah I know." But Dommi wasn't thinking about becoming somebody's underboss. Only for Uncle Mick would he have accepted the number two role because Mick's outfit remained number one. The top of the chain. Which made his number two, his underboss, at the top too. But number two anywhere else would be less than the role of supervising capo he already had with Uncle Mick. He wanted more.

"The Parva syndicate ain't nothing like the Sinatra Crime Family, keeping it real, but we're the biggest in what we do. We're the biggest assassin squad in the country."

"And once I take over," said Dommi, "we'll be the biggest in the world."

"It can happen sooner than you think."

Dommi looked at Archie. "What you talkin' 'bout, Willis?"

Archie laughed at that *Different Strokes* TV show reference. "I heard through the grapevine that if you keep proving how fearless you are like you doing on this assignment, that you'll be running the whole thing within weeks, not months."

Parva had already told Dommi the same thing himself. But that was Dommi's business. "Oh yeah? What grapevine you heard that from?"

"Mr. Parva told me himself when I went to visit him in prison last week. He said you're our best hope for survival if his appeal fails. He said you're tough enough to run the whole thing."

"Why did he put Junior in charge if he didn't think he had what it took?"

"Because Junior was the best he had. But Junior's ass ain't better than yours. Even I know that. And the old man told me that too."

Dommi nodded and smiled. "That's what I'm talking about. He won't regret it." Then he looked at Archie. "What about your ass? You don't wanna be boss?"

"Me? Fuck no! Too much bullshit to

deal with.   Too many people breathing down your neck trying to take your place. I'm an enforcer. That's good enough for me."

Dommi grinned. "And they think you're a fucking college kid on your way to the NFL."

Archie laughed. "I tell people that all the time, and they never once check to see if I'm even enrolled in any college anywhere, which I'm not. But they buy it every time. I even got my own mama snowed into thinking I'm this good college kid soon to make her millions as a big time NFL player."

"How you gonna explain it when it don't come true?"

"Got that planned out too. I'll just tell her I hurt my knee and the NFL gave me severance pay or some insurance policy was cashed in and we're in the big money anyway. I'll buy her a house then and set her up real good. But not yet. I'm not financially there yet."

"Once I get in charge, guys like you will

get their fair share."

Archie stared at Dommi. "I appreciate that, man. I knew you and me were gonna do well together. I liked you when I first met you. And once you finish this job, I'll trust you."

Dommi smiled. "You don't trust me now?"

"You're a Gabrini. We're asking you to handle a Gabrini. No. Not yet."

Dommi looked back down at his uncle. And they both fell into silence.

Until the van pulled off of the road and drove down a back road surrounded by woods. And then the van stopped and Jonah Bark, the driver, got out and opened the back van doors where Dom, Archie, and Sal were housed.

Dommi stood up and looked down at his still unconscious uncle. "You used to believe in me. You knew I had what it took. But you gave up on me too. All you fuckers gave up on me. Even Pops."

Jonah the driver, who worked for the

people that hired the Parva Group to do the job, handed Dommi the loaded gun. Dommi learned quickly, once he joined the Parva Group, that they never used their own weapons on a job. They never provided their own transportation either. They wanted nothing to trace back to Parva.

But Dommi, *being Dommi*, looked at that gun the driver handed him. "What this shit gonna do?" he asked and then angrily tossed it aside. And before the driver could even object, and before Archie could school Dom once again on the rules of hired guns, Dommi had pulled out his own weapon and started firing his weapon as he was yelling at his uncle: "You believe in me now, motherfucker?! Believe in me now?!"

Shot after shot tore through Sal. Even Archie and Jonah were shocked by the viciousness of it, given who Big Sal Gabrini was. And then blood started pooling around Sal's lifeless body.

Dommi was breathing so hard that Archie and Jonah wondered if he was going to be okay.

"Believe in me now?" Dommi said again, but this time with no passion. No emotion. Just words. "Believe in me now?"

Then he suddenly lurched and hurried off of the van. As soon as he got off, he leaned forward and threw up.

Archie, amazed, laughed out loud as he jumped off too. "You did it, Dom!" He was patting him on the back even as Dommi continued to bend over. "You proved yourself this time boy. You iced Big Sal Gabrini! You iced the big dog! Your own uncle. You proved your ass now!"

But Jonah looked livid. Dommi disobeyed the rules. He was a hothead from way back just like he knew he'd be. But that was who they gave the assignment too. What But could he do about it? Stop him? He'd fired before anybody could do anything. Fucking moron! Jonah was inwardly livid. And scared.

But then the man at the parking garage that had driven off with Sal's Bugatti drove up in Sal's car. Archie and Jonah placed Sal's body on the backseat of his own car. Jonah gave instructions on where to leave Sal and that car, and then the Bugatti sped away.

Archie went right back to congratulating Dommi. But Jonah wanted no parts of that bastard. He ordered them to get back in the van so that he could take them to the airport. They needed to get their asses out of Dodge right quick and in a hurry. Once word broke that Sal Gabrini was missing, it was going to be hell to pay.

Besides, the sooner he was done with those two, the better.

And as Archie and Dommi rode in the back of that bloody van, Archie continued to congratulate his partner in crime and talk of all the wonderful things his fearlessness was going to bring to him when Parva found out he completed the job. But Dommi leaned his head back and closed his eyes. He didn't feel fearless at all. He didn't feel tough and powerful the way he expected to feel either.

He just felt bad.

But as Sal's Bugatti traveled in the opposite direction from the van Dommi and Archie were in, the driver of that Bugatti drove without giving that body on that backseat a second glance. But that body on that backseat was still Sal Gabrini. And as that car drove through those backroads of Vegas, Sal's hand began to move. And as it turned corner after corner after corner, Sal's once lifeless tired green eyes began to slowly, but surely, open wide. He couldn't keep them open. He was still too doped up. And he kept falling back asleep. But he was showing some signs, some definite, unmistakable signs, that he wasn't dead yet.

CHAPTER SEVENTEEN

They gathered together in Sal and
Gemma's living room. And everybody sat
there in a state of shock. Tommy and Grace
and their entire family had flown in from
Seattle. Their children, along with all of the
younger members of the family, were ordered
to remain in the family room on the east wing
of the house until further notice, with Jimmy in
charge of the entire group. They didn't want to
alarm the younger set in any way, shape or
form with the alarm they all felt for Sal. They
all knew Sal was in trouble, and there was a
video to confirm that fact. But that was all they
knew. It had been four hours since Sal was
snatched. Four long hours. And they still had

nothing.

But Carmine, being Carmine, had eased his way out of the family room and made his way into his Uncle Sal's home study, and was reviewing that video for himself. Lucky, seeing his cousin ease out, followed him.

Robby was in and out overseeing the drastically increased security around Sal's estate, as all of the top capos in Sal's expansive syndicate converged around the grounds to provide the security themselves. They all, too, had the look of terror on their faces. Somebody snatched *their* boss? Who, they wondered, could ever be that damn daring? They had to either be super-courageous geniuses, they decided amongst themselves, or fools.

Inside the house, Reno was on the phone nonstop, ordering every available man at his disposal to team up with Sal's guys and hit the streets.

Tommy was on the phone nonstop too.

He had flown in a small army of men too, and they were on the streets with the other groups. Tommy wasn't supposed to be in the game anymore, but you wouldn't know it by the company he kept.

Jimmy, whom they all would not allow to ever be connected to that part of the family business, was keeping an eye on those in the family room. He saw his kid brother Carmine sneak out of the room, and Lucky follow him, but that was the level of respect Jimmy had for Carmine's ability to solve puzzles nobody else was able to crack. Lucky had that same kind of respect for Carmine too, even though Carmine was eccentric as hell. But they let Carmine do his thing.

Gemma was seated in the middle of her living room sofa between her daughter Marie and Tommy's wife Grace. Reno's wife Trina was seated in the chair just ending a call.

"Who was that?" Grace asked in her usual quietness that Trina used to hate because it was the direct opposite of her loud, boisterous self. But the men in the family liked that humble quality about Grace, and Tommy loved that she wasn't like the rest of the women of the family, or any woman he'd ever dated. When Tommy first married Grace, Trina used to privately view Grace as Tommy's child because she was *so* differential to him. But they fully respected Grace now, even though she was still differential to Tommy. But she was no shrinking violet. She had grown into her own.

"That was Amelia," Trina said, answering her question. "I wanted her to get a call in to Hammer Reese. But she said she'll try, but don't hold my breath."

"Why not?"

"She said they're separated and barely on speaking terms."

Grace was surprised. "Millie and Hammer have separated? I didn't know that."

"Neither did I," said Trina. "I know

they've been on a rocky road for a long time, but who in our family doesn't have a rocky marriage? I dare you to name one."

"Big Daddy and Jenay," said Gemma.

"Child please," said Trina. "Maybe it's not as rocky now as it used to be, but they've had their knockdown drag outs too."

"Tommy and Grace," Gemma said, squeezing Grace's hand.

"*Tommy and Grace*?" Trina had shock in her voice. "Gemma, are you crazy? They got a divorce before! Remember that? It don't get no rockier than that!"

Grace laughed. "But we remarried," she said. "We're doing great now."

"Why are we talking about this?" asked an agitated Marie. "Daddy's been kidnapped and we're talking about people's relationships? What the fuck is wrong with you people?"

"Now wait a minute, little girl," said Trina. "I know you're worried sick over your father. We all are worried sick. But that doesn't give you a license to speak like your ass our equal. It ain't."

"I know that's right," said Grace.

"I apologize," said Marie. "I'm just so worried!" Then she leaned against Gemma. Gemma, who was so distraught she could barely sit up, placed an arm around her.

Soon, Reno and Tommy sat down on the sofa across from the ladies. They both looked distraught with worry too. And silence ensued.

Until Robby came in with a status update. "Every inch of this property is locked down and secured," he said.

"What about aerial?" asked Tommy. "I ordered aerial security too."

"We took care of that too, sir. We've got two different choppers already hovering around our airspace making sure there are no attacks from above anywhere in the vicinity."

Reno nodded. "Good job, Robby. You're a good number two."

Robby always respected Reno. "Thank you, sir," he said, and then he went back outside to continue to oversee every aspect of the grounds and aerial security.

"He's doing a good job," said Gemma after he left, "but perhaps we should alert the FBI now. It's been hours and we've heard nothing. At least the FBI have boundless resources."

"But their asses aren't about to use a single one of those *boundless resources* to get a reputed mob boss back," said Reno. "Especially not one named Gabrini. There's just no way."

"What about Mick?" asked Trina.

"He's not answering his calls," said Reno. "I called Big Daddy to see if he could get through, but even he couldn't get Mick on the line."

"Big Daddy called," said Gemma. "He wanted to come down, but I told him to wait."

"No sense in coming yet," said Reno.

"We don't know shit yet. What about you, Tommy? You tried to call Uncle Mick yet?"

"Several times. Went to Voice Mail every time."

Reno was surprised. "He wouldn't pick up for you either?"

Tommy shook his head. "Nope."

"I even called Roz," said Reno. "And you know Uncle Mick is going to kick my ass he finds out I bothered his wife. But I couldn't get through to her either."

"What about Hammer Reese?" asked Tommy.

"Trina called Amelia," said Grace, "but she said they're separated and barely on speaking terms."

Tommy pulled out his phone to call Hammer directly. He was able to get through on his first try, which impressed them. But the call was very brief.

"What did he say?" Grace asked.

"He said he's already on it. He said he's

got a BOLO out and a specialized team on the case too."

"But how would he know already?" asked Reno. "Apparently Amelia did get a call through."

But Trina noticed something else. "You guys don't seem surprised by the news."

"What news?" asked Reno.

"That Millie and Hammer are separated and barely on speaking terms."

"Who could be surprised by that?" asked Reno. "Amelia don't wanna give up that gangster life, and Hammer is not the kind of man that's going to tolerate that. I mean think about it, Tree. Here is a man who used to head the CIA and is now in charge of the government's special ops teams. A man many considers the top cop of the land even though he isn't the AG. And as for his wife? Millie could be arrested and brought up on RICO charges on any given day of the week with her gangster ass! It would take a mighty love for that to work out."

"I know that's right," said Marie.

But when she said it, Trina noticed something odd. She noticed that Marie seemed particularly anguished in a strange kind of way. They all were in shock, and filled with anxiety and pure fear for Sal's well-being, but the look on Marie's face took it to another level. "Are you okay?" Trina asked her.

Gemma looked at her daughter too. And she agreed with Trina. Marie looked unwell.

"I'm okay, Auntie," Marie responded to Trina. "I just want Daddy back home safe and sound."

"We all want that," Trina responded. "But you look as if . . ." Trina didn't know the comparison, and didn't want to ruffle anybody's feathers with unfounded suspicion, so she didn't continue.

But Trina and Gemma both noticed that Marie didn't follow it up with the proverbial *I look as if what* usual response.

Marie, instead, stood up. "I'm going to go lay down," she said. "I think I'm just worried too much." She looked at Gemma. "Let me know as soon as you hear something, Ma. Even if I'm sleep, wake me up."

"I will, baby," Gemma said, rubbing her daughter's arm. "And don't worry yourself to death, Marie. He's coming back home to us. I would feel it if it wasn't true."

Marie smiled a weak smile, but that anguish on her pretty face could not be denied. She began to head toward the staircase.

Trina looked at Gemma. "That heifer knows something," she said.

Gemma frowned. "Don't you call my daughter a heifer! And what in the world could she possibly know about Sal's disappearance? Come on now, Tree. She's been out of that gangster life for years."

"But that don't mean she doesn't hear things," said Reno. "All these thugs be around here trying to get in her panties. Even guys at my casino be begging me to set them up with her when I wouldn't set a dog up with those players. And every time I see her she's got a different dude on her arm. She's got the looks of Miss America and the best body in town, and they all know it. And they all want a piece of that sweet ass, let's be clear."

"And let's face it," added Trina, "she likes the bad boys. I'd bet somebody told her something."

"That's ridiculous," Gemma said. But she said it passionlessly. As if she didn't think it was ridiculous at all. As if she knew Marie had a thirst for that life and it wasn't completely out of her system. That was why Trina kept looking at Gemma. She knew Gemma like she knew her name. And just like that, Gemma was on the intercom telling her daughter to get back downstairs.

Marie made it back down in a hurry. "You heard something?" she asked anxiously as she hurried up to her mother. "Daddy's okay?" But she quickly realized everybody was looking at her. "What's wrong?" she asked. "What's happened?"

Gemma took her by the hand. "If you know something, Marie, you have to tell it to us now. It could save your father's life."

"What do you mean?"

"Has anybody told you anything that we need to know about?" asked Reno. "That's what she means."

But instead of saying no, Marie asked a tell-tell question. "Why would you be asking me something like that?"

They all glanced at each other. That wasn't the question an innocent person would ask. That was the question a person trying to get more information would ask. "What your ass hiding?" Reno asked her.

"I'm not hiding anything, Uncle Reno. Why are you asking me these questions?"

"Because you are hiding something,"

said Gemma. "What is it, Marie? Just tell us even if you don't think it matters."

Before Gemma could finish her sentence, Lucky came running into the living area. "Ma! Ma! Carmine found something!"

"Carmine?" asked Reno as they all jumped to their feet. "What are you talking about? What's Carmine's ass got to do with this?"

"He's been looking at that video. He's running programs that allow him to see the faces of those two guys who snatched Pop."

When Lucky said those words, nobody was asking any further questions because they all were running to Sal's home office.

When they got into the office, Carmine was seated behind Sal's desk and had the video on his computer monitor.

"What you got, Carmine?" Gemma, who outran all of them into that office, impatiently asked the young genius.

"I'm getting a clearer and clearer picture

of the two guys who kidnapped Uncle Sal," Carmine responded.

"But how?" asked Tommy, who was brainy too. He put on his glasses and leaned toward the computer screen. "Those ski masks they're wearing conceal their faces from every angle."

"But I'm looking for reflections or mistakes," said Carmine. "I'm not doing angles. There's always a mistake. And here it is!" Carmine was excited. "Here's a clear image of the first one."

And when he pressed that button they saw where the muscular abductor had taken his mask off as he grabbed for the van door that they hadn't closed as the van was speeding away, and he closed it. For that one quick nanosecond Carmine was able to capture the image. And when that face was revealed, everybody in that room gasped in unspeakable shock. They all leaned in at the same time, to get a better look. Even Carmine was leaning in too. And he was floored. "*It can't be*," he said, stunned by his own revelation.

"What the fuck?" said Reno, stunned too.

"No way," said Trina.

Every one of their faces were in a state of profound disbelief.

But Gemma said nothing. Because it was as clear as day. One of the men tossing her husband into the back of that van was none other than Reno and Trina's son Dominic. There was no disputing that reality. There was no spinning that shit.

And she was angry as fuck.

And not a soul in that room would have ever believed it for a million years, or even a billion, had they not been looking at it with their own two eyes.

CHAPTER EIGHTEEN

Reno was so overcome that he had to sit in the chair beside the desk. Trina was so angry that she had already pulled out her phone and was calling their son. Grace and Tommy were just stunned. They knew Dom was impetuous. Everybody knew he could be a hothead and damn reckless when he wanted to be. But nobody would have ever attached his name to Sal's kidnapping!

"How could this be?" Grace asked.

"His *got*damn Voice Mail," Trina said angrily, and ended her call. Then her anger turned to adject horror. She just couldn't believe it.

"What have I done?" Reno was saying, as if he was already blaming himself. "How could my son, *my child*, be a part of something like this?" Then he looked up at Trina.

Trina went to Reno, and they hugged each other.

But Gemma noticed something else. Of all of them, she noticed that Marie seemed the least surprised. "You knew he was involved," she said to her daughter. No more time for beating around the bush. "Didn't you?"

Everybody looked at Marie. Marie didn't deny it, which was guilt to them.

"Tell us what you know?" Trina said to her.

"I don't know anything! Just that I. . ."

Reno hurried over to her. "Just that you what?"

"I heard that Dommi was doing his own thing. That he was no longer working for Uncle Mick and cousin Teddy."

This shocked them all. Reno was frowning. It was news to him too. "Who told you that? Dommi?"

"No," said Marie. "I haven't spoken to Dommi in weeks."

"Then who told you?"

"Mariah told me."

"Is she here?" asked Reno. "She and the baby are here, right?"

"They're in the family room," said Lucky.

"Go get her," Reno ordered, and Lucky took off.

"What else did she tell you?" Gemma asked her daughter.

205

"That's all."

"Don't fuck with us, Marie," Reno said, "or I'll kick your natural ass."

"That's all she told me, Uncle Reno. I didn't know he was a part of any of this or I would have said something. I just thought, because he didn't work for Uncle Mick anymore, that he might have gotten mixed up with the wrong crowd. That's all. I don't know any more than you do. I'm just worried about my daddy!"

Gemma pulled her into her arms. "It's alright, baby," she said as Marie sobbed.

Then Carmine's voice echoed through the tension. "Here's the second guy," he said. After his own initial shock of uncovering his own brother in the scheme, he had continued to work on the images. "He's coming clear now."

They all gathered around the computer again. Reno and Trina looked especially hard, figuring the second guy to be a friend of

Dommi's. To be somebody they may also recognize. "Is he familiar to anybody?" Carmine asked when the image became clear.

But Reno and Trina were both shaking their heads. "Never seen him before," said Trina.

"Me neither," said Reno.

Tommy and Grace had never seen him before either.

"What about you, Marie?" asked Trina.

But Marie was a negative too. "I don't know him."

The only person who had not said a word was Gemma. Because she was in a state of shock when that second person was revealed. She didn't have to look hard at all to know who the second kidnapper was.

She removed her reading glasses and moved in even closer. Just in case she was hallucinating.

But it was no hallucination. She wished to God it was, but it wasn't. And her heart began hammering.

Then she quickly looked up, at everybody, as if she was already exposed.

CHAPTER NINETEEN

She knew she had to tell it and tell it all. As soon as she realized who the second kidnapper was, for Sal's sake she knew she could keep silent no longer. But the memories flooded back, and the pain of that day, and she couldn't bear it. But she had to. For Sal.

But Mariah and Lucky came into the office.

"Mariah," said Reno, hurrying over to her.

"Lucky said you guys wanted to see me."

"We need to know about Dommi," said Reno as they all gathered around Mariah.

"What about Dommi?"

"Marie said you told her something was going on with him. Something big."

"I don't know anything for sure, Dad, but

I overheard him talk about leaving Uncle Mick."

"Leaving his organization?"

Mariah nodded. "Yes, sir."

"Did he say where he was going if he left Uncle Mick?"

"No sir. But he talked like he had something laid out for him. Something really big. He just didn't say what it was in that one conversation I overheard."

"Who was he talking to?" asked Tommy. "Do you know?"

"No sir. It just concerned me that he was leaving Uncle Mick."

"Why would that concern you?"

"Because you know how Dommi can be. That's why you guys moved him from under Uncle Sal and placed him under Uncle Mick. He knows Uncle Mick will kill him if he goes rogue, family or no family. Just like what Uncle Mick did to his own son."

"You don't know nothing about that," Reno was quick to point out. What happened to Mick Sinatra's oldest son Adrian was a family secret never to be revealed. Dommi, apparently, revealed it to Mariah.

"Don't worry, Dad. My child is a blood Gabrini. I would never tell."

"Your ass just told us," said Reno. "You keep that shit out of your mouth."

"Yes, sir."

"Is that all you were concerned about, Mariah?" Tommy asked.

"Yes, sir. I begged him not to leave Uncle Mick. I told him he would be playing with fire if he betrayed Uncle Mick. I even threatened to tell you, Dad. But he made me swear not to. He said it was just talk and nothing more. But now I hear he may be involved in what happened to Uncle Sal." Tears appeared in her eyes.

"It's okay, baby," Trina said to her as she gave her a quick hug. "Just go back to the family room. We're taking care of it."

"Is Dommi alright? I've been trying to

text him and call him but I get no responses. Is he in trouble?"

Trina was no liar. "If he's involved in this shit, then yes. He's in the kind of trouble he's never been in before."

"I don't' know how much of this I can take, Ma. It's always something with Dommi."

Trina pulled her into her arms again. Then she pulled back from her. "Stop worrying. We're handling it, okay? Just go back into the family room and let us do what we need to do." She looked at Marie. "Stay with her, Marie."

Marie went over and placed an arm around Mariah.

"But you'll let me know if you hear from Dommi?"

"I sure will," Trina assured her, Mariah nodded, and then she and Marie headed back to the family room.

"You go with them, Lucci," said Tommy. And Lucky left the office too.

"Lord, Lord," said Trina, her hand on the side of her face. Her heart was all over the place. How in the world could a child she birth be mixed up in a kidnapping of his beloved uncle? It seemed crazy to her! And for Mariah to have to suffer too? She was going to kick Dommi's ass when she got a hold of that fool.

But what if it was true?

Then before she could even consider that possibility, Gemma dropped another bombshell.

"I know the second kidnapper," she said quickly, before she lost her nerve again. And everything stopped.

And everybody looked at her. "You know him?" asked Reno.

Gemma nodded, her face devastated.

"Who is he?"

She had to steel herself just to say his name again. "Archie Jefferson."

Tommy could see her devastation. He provided a chair for her to sit down. And once she sat down, she told all about that fateful day in that game room. She left nothing out.

When she finished talking, you could hear a feather fly. It was just that quiet. Even Reno, who'd seen it all, was devastated for Gemma. But nobody knew what to say. Nobody knew how to equate that day with what happened to Sal. Nobody knew how to equate that day with Dommi. Nobody knew what to do!

But before they could fully process the bomb she had just laid on them, or even formulate some nexus, Robby flung open the office door. "We just spotted Sal's car!" he yelled out and every one of them, led by Gemma, didn't wait for details. They took off running.

CHAPTER TWENTY

They piled into an SUV and a convoy of SUVs sped out of the security gate and traveled two blocks away, where Sal's Bugatti, tucked back in an alleyway, was parked.

Some of Sal's capos, who took off as soon as they got word of the sighting, were already there and running up to his Bugatti like teenagers at a rock concert. He barely was able to step out of the car before they were hugging him and patting him on the back and giving each other high-fives. The boss was back! It was Sal Gabrini in the flesh. And they had to press his flesh to believe it.

Like most mob bosses, Sal was a very feared man. His capos knew without a shadow of a doubt that Sal would *grave* your ass if you did him wrong. But unlike most bosses, Sal was beloved by his syndicate and even the affiliate organizations too. Because they all saw Sal as a good man: a man with heart and a moral core. There were lines he wouldn't cross unless you crossed him. He didn't have a tyrannical bone in his body.

Sal was happy to see his guys too. After his hours-long ordeal, he was glad to be back too.

"Sal!"

When he heard that voice among all the voices surrounding him, he pushed away from his guys and turned and looked. And that was when he saw Gemma running toward him. And as soon as he saw that wonderful face he loved so much, he tore away from his guys and ran to her. She was the one he wanted. All those gorgeous females who were constantly trying to get dick from him was a source of great frustration for him. He was a man's man with an oversized sexual appetite. But every time he saw Gemma again, *his* Gemma, it reminded him of what the sacrifice was all about. It was about her. And their family. It was worth every turn down.

Gemma couldn't get to Sal fast enough. Her friends were always questioning his fidelity. Always questioning how a man like him, the second most powerful mob boss in the country no less, and a very nice-looking guy, could ever be a one-woman man. Her own mind sometimes questioned it too. But what she never questioned was his love for her and their children. That was never up for debate she didn't care what they said. That was why it stung her so when she saw that video. She realized how blessed she was to have a man like Sal. She realized it the entire time he was missing how blessed she was that he chose her above all those women he could have chosen. And now he was back. And right in front of her. She fell into his arms.

Sal's men were grinning and looking at each other as the boss, once again, revealed his weakness for that one particular person. Many of them didn't see it: what was so special about her that she would win the Sal Gabrini sweepstakes? They'd been wondering for years. But they could wonder for decades because Sal didn't give a shit. He knew why Gemma was the one.

She was the one who pulled back from their embrace first. Because she needed to see his face and touch his body and make certain he was okay.

But Gemma immediately saw what looked like residue on his face and chest. "What's that on your forehead," she asked, "and your chest?" Then she panicked. "Oh, Sal, and there's blood!"

"What? Where?" Tommy turned Sal

toward him.

"I saw that too, in the car," Sal said as Tommy inspected him. "But it's not my blood. Something sure as hell happened. I don't know what. But I'm okay."

Reno was looking at the residue too. And the blood. "If it's not yours, then who the fuck is it?"

"How should I know? I woke up in my car with this shit all over me."

Then Tommy started looking around. "Let's get out of here. We still don't know what the fuck is going on."

But they were all far more happy than they had been. Especially Gemma. Sal was back! That was all she needed to know.

Reno and Trina, however, still had a son out there. A son who was a part of Sal's abduction. They needed to know a whole lot more than that.

CHAPTER TWENTY-ONE

When the convoy of SUVs drove through the gate, Lucky and Marie were running out of the house toward them. When Sal saw his two oldest children, he hopped out and ran to them.

"Dad!" Dad!" they were crying as he ran to them.   And when they met, he embraced first Marie, and then Lucky, and then both of them together. And Sal was emotional for the first time. He wanted to see his baby too. Then he could exhale. Gemma came up to them, so happy she was in tears as well, and he embraced her too.

As they made their way into the house, his children were asking about the residue and blood on their father too. But when they realized it wasn't their father's blood, they were okay.

But as Reno and Trina made it back into the house, they were still devastated. They were happy beyond measure to see Sal alive and well. That was the most important thing. But Dommi was involved? *Their* son would kidnap his own uncle like that? And what if that blood was Dommi's blood? What if they wanted him to do something to Sal he wouldn't do, and they took Dommi out? They were still reeling. They were still trying to wrap their brains around what had become of their son!

But Reno, being Reno, took charge. "Let's get him inside," he finally said, looking around again to make sure there was no sneak attack on the horizon.

But Sal looked at Reno, his sworn nemesis and best friend and favorite cousin all wrapped into one. "Get him inside? You make me sound like a boy toy!"

The others laughed, although Reno was

still too shook up to go that far, as the two men hugged too. And then the family went inside. Robby remained outside to ensure that the joyous capos didn't let their guards down, and returned to their posts.

After Sal went into the family room to hold his baby girl Teresa and to embrace Jimmy and the rest of the younger set, and after fielding a call from Big Daddy, who was thrilled to have him back among the living, he returned to the living room. He sat on the sofa in between Gemma and Tommy, with Reno sandwiched between Trina and Grace on the second sofa. These three couples were the power center of the Gabrini dynasty, and they all were waiting with bated breath for Sal to tell them where on earth did those bastards take him.

"I have no idea," said Sal as they all were sitting on the edge of their seats, including Sal. They told him what was on the video. But he could recall very little. "I remembered some fucker knocking me out in that parking garage where Hawkins lived."

Gemma was surprised. "Judge Hawkins? What were you doing there?"

"He talked to you like you was a pile of shit in that restaurant. What do you think?"

Gemma was again surprised. "You were at Gateshead?"

Sal hated to admit it. "Yeah."

"Why?"

"Curtis said you were going to meet some old friends you hadn't seen in years. I didn't know those bitches from a hole in the wall. I had to make certain it wasn't some setup. Then Hawkins showed up."

"Makes you wonder if that was the set up," said Tommy.

Sal pointed at Tommy as if he hit the nail on the head.

"But what happened while you were with them?" asked Reno. "Did you see faces?"

"No faces," said Sal. "Don't even

remember any voices. It was morning when they snatched me. But now it's what? Afternoon?"

"They had you for over five hours," said Gemma.

"But I don't remember one second after they knocked me out. When I woke back up, I was in my car in that fucking alley just a couple blocks from my house."

"We got guys getting video from every business in that area. We hope to find out who left you there because you didn't drive yourself there."

"No way. I would have remembered that."

"But you said there's video? Were you able to identify those fuckers? Was it anybody we know?"

Everybody looked at each other. Nobody wanted to tell him, but he could sense there was something to tell.

"Okay, let's have it," Sal said. "Don't

hold any shit back. Just tell me. I can take it."

They didn't know where to begin. Maybe Gemma should go first. But Gemma looked mortified.

So Reno took charge. "Robby and me were able to secure the video from that parking garage."

Sal was hopeful. "Which means you saw those fuckers?"

"Only after Carmine worked his magic," said Tommy.

Sal frowned. "*Carmine*?"

"They wore ski masks," said Trina. "But Carmine was able to see a quick glimpse of their faces and make their grainy images clear."

Sal shook his head. "That Carmine. I thought Tommy was the brains of the family. Carmine takes it to another level. "So what did he find out?"

"The first guy we all know," said Tommy.

"Yeah? Who is he? Who's that

motherfucker?"

They all looked at Reno. Reno frowned. "It was Dominic, Sal."

Sal just stared at Reno. He had to have heard him wrong. "Dominic? *Our* Dommi?"

Reno nodded his head with such a look of regret on his face that it broke Sal's heart. "Are you telling me, Reno, that our Dommi was one of the guys that snatched me?"

"He wasn't the one that hit you," said Reno, quick to point out, "but yes, he was one of the two that grabbed you and threw you in a van."

Sal could hardly believe it. He and Dommi were close. It was Sal that Reno and Trina chose for Dommi to come to work with when he refused to leave that gangster life alone. It couldn't be true.

Somethings he had to see to believe. Dommi even thinking about doing him harm was one of those things.

He stood up. "Where's the video?" he

asked nobody in particular. "I need to see that video."

"It's in your office," said Tommy, and Sal began making his way to his office. Tommy placed his arm around Grace and they all followed Sal.

And as Sal watched that video, you could hear a pin drop. And when he finished, he moved over to the wall behind his desk and leaned against it.

Reno exhaled. "Apparently he left Uncle Mick and holed up with some other group. We don't know who yet."

Sal looked at Reno. "What does Uncle Mick say?"

Tommy exhaled. "We haven't been able to reach him."

Sal frowned. "What are you talking? My ass goes missing for hours, and he's too busy to pick up his phone?"

Tommy and Reno glanced at each other.

"I'd bet he'd pick it up if it was you, or even Reno. But my slick ass? He's too busy."

"It's not like that, Sal, and you know it," said Tommy. "He's probably working the case as we speak."

Sal wasn't trying to hear that. "What about the other guy? Who's that? Anybody recognize him?"

Gemma's heart was racing. She knew she could hold back no longer. And given Sal's volatility after finding out Dommi was involved, she knew she had to tell it in front of Reno and Tommy. Because Sal might not want to have anything more to do with her when he found out, and they would be there to hold him up.

"Yes," she said, and everybody looked at her.

"Yes what?" asked Sal.

"I know who the second person is."

"*You* know him? How would you know a fucker like that?"

There was no way to say it pleasantly, so Gemma decided to just say it. "He raped me."

A loud gasp of shock filled the room. Sal unfolded his arms and stood up from his leaned position. And a fixed frown was on his face. "He *raped* you? What are you talking, Gemma? Somebody raped you while I was missing?"

"No, Sal," said Trina. "That's not what she means."

Sal's heart was pounding. "Then what do you mean?" he asked his wife as he stared at her.

Gemma was fighting back tears, but she was determined to tell it all. "It happened three months ago, Sal, not today. We launched an appeal on a case, and the appeal failed. Miss Bettye's son."

"Miss Bettye? That old bat that works around your office?"

"Sal!" said Trina.

"I don't mean nothing by it, Tree, damn! She seems like a nice lady. But is that the one you're talking about, Gemma?"

"She used to come in and clean up the offices in my law firm, yes. She's the one. She quit after . . . After it happened."

"After the appeal failed?" asked Sal. He was still confused.

"After the assault."

"Babe, you aren't making any sense. What are you talking? Her son, your client, assaulted you because you lost the case?"

"Donte remained locked up," said Gemma. "It wasn't that son. It was Archie, her older son."

Sal's heart began to pound. "What happened?"

"I went over to the house to personally let Miss Bettye know that we lost the appeal, but nobody was home except for Archie. He told me he was in the game room and to come on back."

Sal's jaw tightened.

"I've gone back there many times, so I didn't think anything of it. She hesitated. She could see Sal's entire demeanor changing.

"Go on," said Tommy. "Just tell him, Gem. He has to know."

Gemma steeled herself. "When I went back there, and told him the news, he broke down crying and I tried to comfort him. But then he started acting like . . . . He threw me on the bed and the next thing I know he was . . . he was . . ."

"But you stopped it right?" asked Sal. "You got that motherfucker off of you, right?"

"I tried, Sal. With everything within me I tried. And I did beat his ass. But I was only able to do it after he . . . did that to me."

They were all still stunned by the news themselves. And they looked at Sal. The men especially were concerned. The idea that one of their wives would not have fought that bastard off before it happened was too terrifying for them to even imagine. How could Sal?

Tears were falling from Gemma's eyes as she saw the pain all over Sal's face. It was bad enough. Now this too? "I tried to stop him, Sal. But I just couldn't. He was too strong."

Sal's heart was hammering. They teach their women how to fight off an attacker. That was the first thing a Gabrini lady learned how to do. But Gemma wasn't able to do it? *His strong Gemma*? A part of him was angry at her.

But that was a minor part. The rest of him was anguished for her. And he hurried to his wife and pulled her into his arms. No way was that her fault! "It's alright, baby," he said to her. "It's alright."

She sobbed in his arms. And they all remained silent because they understood the agony of it. But then Sal pulled her back, placed his arms on her small shoulders, and looked at her. "You did nothing wrong," he said to her. "You hear me? It was done to you. You didn't do that shit to nobody. Don't you dare blame yourself."

Gemma's heart felt relieved for the first time since it happened. "Thank you, Sal."

"But Gemma," Sal said, his voice revealing his anguish, "why didn't you tell me when it first happened?"

"Because of Miss Bettye. It would have killed her. She had a heart attack right there in my office when she found out that Donte's appeal failed. Imagine what it would have done to her if she found out that the only child she had left was a rapist? And had raped me? And I know what you would have done to Archie if you ever found out."

"Damn right," said Reno. "Sal would have killed his ass, then me and Tommy would have killed him too."

Trina rolled her eyes. That made no kind of sense! But they all understood what

Reno meant.

"And that's why I couldn't tell you or anybody else in the family," said Gemma. "For Miss Bettye's sake. I couldn't do that to that sweet, poor woman."

"So you carried that burden and allowed that bastard to roam free for three whole months?"

Gemma nodded. "Yes."

"That's why you been in that funk you've been in for the last three months," said Sal, realizing the connection.

Gemma nodded. "Yes. I didn't want to believe that was the reason. Once I made up my mind to take that day to my grave, there was no turning back for me. But it kept coming back in my dreams. And sometimes I would see a man who looked like Archie, and get chills. Or I'd just get down in the dumps and not be able to get myself out of it so easily. But I refused to believe it was what happened that day. I had swept that under a rug never to be overturned again. I didn't want to believe it. But it wouldn't leave me alone."

Sal pulled her into his arms again, but Gemma pulled back. The fact that Sal understood strengthened her. She knew they had to get on with it. "Archie," she said, "is the second guy."

"I let Robby know while we were riding over to your car," said Tommy. "We've got everybody humanly possible looking not just for Dommi, but for Archie Jefferson too."

"I want that fucker alive," said Sal. "Nobody's taking him out but me."

"I told Robby that too. He passed the word."

"We want them both alive," said Reno.

"They know not to touch Reno Gabrini's kid."

As he said it, one of their phones began to ring. Only after several rings did Gemma realize it was Sal's phone in her suit coat pocket. She pulled it out and looked at the

Caller ID. She then handed it to Sal.

"Who is it?" Reno asked.

"Uncle Mick," said Gemma, and they all wanted to hear that conversation.

"Put it on Speaker," said Tommy.

Sal answered the call, placing it on Speaker. "Uncle Mick, hey. You won't believe the kind of day we've been having."

But to think he wouldn't already know, Sal suddenly realized, was foolhardy. "My plane in at the airport," Mick said. "Get on it."

Sal frowned. "What do you mean? We have our own planes."

But Tommy was closest to Mick Sinatra. He knew, if Mick wanted them on his plane specifically, there was a reason. "Who all do you want on the plane?" Tommy asked him. "Just Sal?"

Mick didn't hesitate. "Salvatore," he said, "and everybody."

CHAPTER TWENTY-TWO

It was a five-hour flight from Vegas to Philly and everybody had settled into their own space on Mick Sinatra's massive jet.

They did as they were ordered and all of the Gabrinis were on that plane: all of Tommy and Grace's children. Sal and Gemma's children. Jimmy's daughter and Oprah, and all of Reno and Trina's children. Except for Dominic. Which was why Reno and Trina, like Sal and Gemma, had retired to one of the bedrooms on Mick's plane, to decompress and deal privately with the reality of what they'd seen. While the younger people were in the back of the plane, Jimmy took a break and were in the bedroom with his parents.

"How's Mariah holding up?" Trina asked. She and Reno were on their backs lying on top of the bed.

"She's managing," Jimmy said. He was laying sideways across the bed at their feet. "We all figure it must be true if Uncle Mick is ordering all of us to Philly."

"I wouldn't call it an order," said Trina.

"I would," said Reno. "Jimmy got it right. He might be a business mogul now thanks to Tommy promoting him to be his number two, but he's still got that Gabrini street smarts. And he knows this shit serious. Dommi has apparently left Uncle Mick and took up with some rival group."

But it was still amazing to Jimmy. "He knows how Uncle Mick is. What I don't understand is who would be on that kind of level that Dom would risk it, Pop?"

Reno shook his head. "Hell if I know. But we not only have to find his ass before Mick does--"

"if Mick hasn't already found him," said Trina.

"Right," agreed Reno. "And then we got to stop Mick from killing his ass before we can kill him ourselves!"

Jimmy shook his head. "I still don't believe it, Pop. Dommi kidnap Uncle Sal? He loves Uncle Sal. He wouldn't do that to family. And that blood they found on Uncle Sal?"

Reno exhaled. "That's worrying us too. But that video wasn't lying, thanks to Carmine's smart ass."

"Don't you dare blame Carmine," said Trina. "He only revealed the truth. We just don't wanna accept the truth."

Reno and Jimmy glanced at each other. And then silence fell upon that bedroom like an overcast sky because both men knew she wasn't lying.

In the master bedroom, baby Teresa was asleep in her bassinet while Sal and

Gemma were in Mick's bed, on their sides, facing each other. Dommi's involvement was bad enough. But to Sal it paled in comparison to the news Gemma had laid on him. "Don't you ever do that again," he said to her.

Gemma stared at him. Did he have a change of heart? Now that they were in private, was he blaming her? "Don't ever do what again?"

"Don't you ever keep a secret like that from me ever again, Gemma, you hear me? If shit goes down, you tell me and let those motherfucking chips fall where they may. A man's gonna assault my wife and still walk above ground on this earth? That ain't never gonna happen again. You hear me?"

"I hope I don't get assaulted again, Sal, but yes, I hear you."

Sal stared at her. Then he placed his hand on the side of her face. "You have a big heart, Gem. I know you were worried about Miss Bettye. I understand why you did it. But don't you get it?"

"Get what?"

Sal hated to admit it, since it wouldn't help him any, but he felt he had to say it for her sake alone. "Don't you understand the power you have over me?"

Gemma was shocked to hear him phrase it that way. "What power?"

"If you would have insisted that I don't kill that fool, I wouldn't have. I would have beat his ass to within an inch of his life, but you and you alone might have been able to persuade me to leave it at that."

"Number one, you're lying," said Gemma. "Just like you said before that lie, there was no way you were going to let a man do that to me and still walk the face of this earth. Number two, even if I believe you and you did beat him up and left him alone, then Reno and Tommy would have took it from there. And if they didn't, then Uncle Mick or Big Daddy would have. Boy please. I know this family like the back of my hand."

Sal couldn't help but smile. Then he rubbed her soft, dark skin again. Then his look turned somber again. "I'm just sorry you had to suffer alone. All those months. But I understand why you did it."

"But what I don't understand is how Archie and Dommi could have gotten together. I don't see how they could have known each other."

"We're about to find out," said Sal, pulling Gemma into his arms. "If anybody knows, Uncle Mick already does."

"I wonder why he wanted the whole family with us," said Gemma.

"I'm wondering about that myself. Something's up. And it's big or he would have never sent his own plane and ordered us to bring everybody. Something bad's going down, Gemma. Something rotten to the core. I can feel it in my bones. And it's got everything to do with that damn Dommi."

"But what about him?"

Sal shook his head. "I don't know. Never could figure that kid out. But whatever it is, it's bad."

Gemma looked at Sal, worried too. Because Sal's intuition was never wrong. And she held him even tighter.

CHAPTER TWENTY-THREE

The plane landed at a private Philadelphia airport and Teddy Sinatra, Mick's son and the head of the Sinatra Crime Family, along with Teddy's wife Nikki, his underboss, boarded the plane as the Gabrinis were ready to get off.

"Welcome to Philly everybody," Teddy said to his relatives.

"What's the plan, Ted?" Reno asked him.

"You, Sal, and your wives will go with Nikki. Everybody else goes with me and Uncle Tommy."

That surprised Reno and Sal. "Tommy?" Reno asked.

But Gemma, who was holding Teresa in her arms, was concerned. "We have our baby with us. Surely she can stay with Sal and I."

"She's going to the safe house with everybody else," Teddy said as if he was the boss of them.

Which offended Sal and Reno mightily. "Says who? You?" Sal quickly asked. "When your ass got ahead of me?"

"When I took over Pop's syndicate," Teddy fired back.

Although Mick was still very much in charge, Teddy was the new face of the organization. And since the Sinatra Crime Family was and would always be the number one syndicate in the world, that by rights made Teddy number one. But not in the eyes of any major boss on the planet. Mick still ran that show. Sal's syndicate was still number two. Teddy was number three, muscling out Monk Paletti and forcing him down a notch. They would give Teddy the number three slot. But no higher than that.

And Teddy understood that. "But I get it, Uncle Sal, alright? I'm just here to help."

"And we thank you for your help Teddy," said Trina. "You too, Nikki. Don't mind Beavis and Butthead. They wanna be in charge of everything and everybody with their stupid selves. We're on your turf now. You run this and don't you forget it."

Teddy and Nikki smiled. "Yes, ma'am," said Teddy.

"Listen to Trina if you want," warned Sal.

"What's the plan?" Reno asked.

"Like I said, you and Uncle Sal and your wives will go with Nikki. Everybody else will go with Uncle Tommy and me."

"And don't worry about Teresa, Gem," Grace said. "I'll be in charge of her."

Gemma smiled and handed the baby over to Grace. "Thanks, Grace. I just don't understand why she can't come with us." She looked at Teddy and Nikki. "Isn't Roz at home?"

"Nope," said Nikki. "Boss ordered her and the twins to the safe house too."

"Why didn't Teddy order it?" asked Reno.

"Because Roz is under Pop's command," Teddy responded. "Not mine."

"Yeah I thought so," said Reno. "Mick will kick your ass you try to order his wife around. And that goes double from me if you try to order my ass around. You feel me?"

Teddy glanced at Nikki. These OGs will never change! "Yes, Uncle Reno, I feel you."

"And when did Tommy get in the mix?" asked Sal. He looked at his older brother. "You knew they had you in charge of the safe house crew with Teddy?"

Tommy nodded. "Yes."

"Since when?" asked Reno.

"Since we've been on this plane. Uncle Mick called me."

"Why am I not surprised?" Reno shook his head. "He's always singling you out like you're our boss! Why does he always put you in charge of security?"

"Maybe because I'm a security expert?" Tommy answered. "Maybe because I own and have owned for decades a security firm?"

"Or maybe you're just his favorite and he never wants you in the mud," said Sal.

Reno pointed at Sal in agreement. "That answer," he said.

"Let's get this show on the road, folks," said Teddy, and they all began getting off the plane.

Even Reno and Sal had to admit that the level of security was outstanding, as capos from Mick and Teddy's organization met them at the air steps and escorted them like a blanket of protection to the waiting SUVs. Ten SUVs in all. Sal and Gemma and Reno and Trina, along with Nikki, got in the third SUV. The Gabrini children and baby Teresa in Grace's arms, and Tommy and Teddy, got in the fifth and sixth SUVs. Those two SUVs, along with four others, took off in a straight line heading to the safe house. The third SUV, along with the first and second and fourth SUVs, took off for Mick's house.

Nikki was seated on the front seat with the driver. Trina and Gemma were seated on the third row. Reno and Sal were on the backseat.

Sal leaned forward. "What's this all about, Nick? Why did your father-in-law summon all of us here?"

"You know as much as I know, Uncle Reno."

"I doubt that shit."

"I'm telling you Pop ordered me and Teddy to get to this airport and oversee the transport. That's all he would tell us, and you know Teddy asked him repeatedly for more info. But he didn't give it to him."

"And he thinks his ass running this organization?"

Nikki looked out of the window. "He knows he's not," she said. "Even our capos are giving him a hard time."

Reno and Sal glanced at each other. "What is he doing about it?" Sal asked.

"He's kicking ass, and so am I. That's what we're doing."

"I know that's right," said Reno.

"And take names," said Sal. "They continue to buck your authority, you get rid of those assholes. Teddy can't have that."

The irony wasn't lost on Nikki. Gemma either. "*They* buck his authority and that's okay," Gemma said. "But let anybody else do it, and they got a problem with that."

Nikki laughed. "My sentiments exactly."

But when the laughter ceased, reality returned. And it was an unwelcomed intruder. "Is it true about my son?" Reno decided to ask Nikki.

Nikki's heart squeezed at just the thought of it. Dommi had been doing so well, she thought. But that was for Pop to explain. "Whatever do you mean?" she responded.

Reno shook his head. "Uncle Mick got

your ass well-trained."

Nikki tried to smile, but thinking about Dommi dampened that for her too. They continued riding in silence.

And then *BAM*!!!

It was so powerful it rocked their SUV.

"Motherfuck!" cried Reno as the second SUV directly in front of them was hit by an improvised explosive device and the front end lifted up and then the entire vehicle exploded.

"Get out of formation now!" Nikki ordered the driver as their SUV swerved out of formation and the driver hit the gas metal.

"Get down, Gem and Tree!" Sal yelled as the ladies got down and the men were pulling their weapons and looking out of the windows.

"Where are those fuckers?" Reno was asking.

"Over there!" Nikki said as she spotted the truck on the side of the road much further up. A man standing outside of the truck had a launcher in his hand. They pressed down windows and started shooting in rapid succession, but not before the man by the truck got off another homemade bomb. That IED hit the first SUV, causing it to buckle and then explode too, even as it was trying to get out of formation.

"Get that fucker!" Reno was yelling, and he and Nikki were doing just that. But Sal moved to the windows on the other side to make sure there was no backside attack.

He instinct was spot on. An SUV was speeding up on the outer side of their SUV and a group of gunmen were just getting ready to fire on the third SUV. But Sal leaned out of the window and started firing in such rapid and accurate succession that the driver had to swerve to avoid getting hit. He got hit anyway, and so did the two front tires. The men were trying to shoot back, but the driver was dead and the SUV lost control. It lost traction, flew over a ditch, and slammed into the side of the embankment, exploding on contact.

The third and fourth SUVs kept going. But everybody remained on alert, looking around and checking side roads and making sure they weren't still under attack.

Nikki was already on her phone frantically calling Teddy to make sure the convoy of SUVs heading to the safe house weren't suffering a similar fate.

CHAPTER TWENTY-FOUR

"I don't like this, Mick."

Mick Sinatra was in his home office leaned on the front side of his desk, his long legs outstretched. In black pants and a black turtleneck, his big, muscular body filled the space. His wife Roz was on the other end of the phone. And she was giving him a mouthful.

"You know I don't like this shit. I don't see why I had to come to some safe house anyway. Why couldn't I stay home?"

"Because I said you couldn't."

"I don't need to be here. Why I got to be here? I can take care of myself."

"You'd better take care of yourself and my children, too. And you're going to do so at that safe house. Because that's where your ass is staying until I tell you differently."

"Fuck you, Mick!"

"Behave yourself and do what they tell you to do, Roz, or you'll do more than fuck me. You'll hear from my ass. And you won't like that conversation."

"You bastard!" she yelled and hung up in his face. He angrily tossed his phone across his desk. And then his office door flew open and two of his capos hurried in.

"The convoy was attacked, Boss."

"Attacked?" Mick was shocked. "Which one? The one heading for the safe house?"

"Nikki's convoy."

Mick began hurrying toward the exit, pointing as he hurried. The second capo, seeing what the boss was pointing at, grabbed the shotgun on a side table and tossed it to him. Mick caught it and then he and the two capos hurried out of his office and out of the house.

The third and fourth SUVs were

speeding through the security gate when Mick
and his capos made it outside. Security was
super-tight around the vast Sinatra compound
as they hurried to the third SUV. Nikki and the
Gabrinis were getting out.

"Any losses?" Mick asked Nikki.

"Two SUVs. Eight of our men dead."

"Motherfuck!" Mick yelled angrily. "What
about the second convoy?"

"I called Ted," said Nikki. "They made it
to the safe house with no problems. But we
got problems, Pop. That was too easy."

Mick knew it too. He began hurrying
back toward the house. Sal and Gemma and
Reno and Trina, along with Nikki, hurried
behind him.

Mick didn't stop until he hurried back in
his office, sitting his shotgun back on the side
table, and pressed a button that opened a full
wall. That wall was a closet with an extensive
wardrobe of long white coats and black
trousers and black turtlenecks, and guns of

every conceivable kind: long, short, fat, thin. Mick, already in black pants and a black turtleneck, grabbed one of his white coats and began putting it on.

Sal opened up one of the coats and motioned toward Reno. Reno moved over and they both saw how it was decked down with weaponry.

"*Damn*," said Reno. They were both shocked. Now they fully understood why Mick always wore those coats in battle.

But when Mick pressed a button and closed the wall-like closet once again, and began heading out of the office, Sal moved in front of every one of them. "Uncle Mick?" he was saying as they all continued to try and keep up with the fast-moving Mick the Tick. "*Uncle Mick?*"

When Mick wouldn't respond to Sal, he grabbed Mick by the arm and turned him around.

Everybody stopped. They were scared

for Sal. Especially with that chilling look on Mick's face and the way he looked down at Sal's hand on his arm.

Sal removed his hand from Mick, but he didn't back down. "You asked us to come here, and we came. We nearly died after we got here. We have a right to know what the fuck is going on!"

"Sal's right," said Reno, stepping forward too. "Meaning no disrespect, Uncle Mick, but Nikki said it best. That ambush was too easy. You asked us to come here. But what the fuck is happening? And how did my son manage to get involved in this shit?"

Mick stared at both of them, and he stared for a long time. Then he spoke. "I didn't ask," he said.

"Okay, fine," said Sal, stunned that he would go there. "You *told* us to come. Alright? That better? But why, Uncle Mick? What's going on?"

"Is it Dominic?" asked Reno.

Mick pinched the bridge of his nose and closed his eyes. It was the first time the family had seen him look that stressed-out in a long time. They looked at each other. Even Nikki was concerned. Then Mick made his way into the living room and sat down in the chair. He motioned and they all sat down too.

"Dominic is no longer with my syndicate," Mick said.

"Since when?" asked Reno.

"Since about a month ago."

They were all shocked. Especially Reno. "*A month ago*? That's bullshit! He was working for you a month ago."

"For me, yes, but for Danny Parva too. He was playing both ends."

Sal frowned. "Danny Parva? *Got*damn!"

"Who's Danny Parva?" asked Trina, her anguish growing with every new revelation. Even though she and Gemma had spoken to everybody at the safe house to ensure they and the baby were all okay, the sting of that attack, and the fact that it happened on Mick's turf, rattled them. Who were these people? And Dommi could be involved with them? Trina was in bad shape.

Mick saw it too. Once upon a time she was his gold standard in the female category. He was very attracted to her. He still respected her.

"Who's Danny Parva, Mick?" she asked again.

But Reno shook his head. "You don't wanna know, babe," he said to his wife.

But that only made Trina more anxious. "Are you saying Dommi's mixed up with him?" Trina asked Mick.

Mick exhaled. "Yes."

Gemma looked at her husband. "Who is he, Sal? Just tell us!"

Sal didn't want to, but they had a right to know. "Danny Parva runs the most powerful assassin syndicate in the country."

"*Assassin syndicate*?" asked Trina. "You mean a hit man squad?"

"Yes. They're hired guns. Parva went to prison four months ago on racketeering charges. His son took over three months ago and started recruiting Dommi as one of his capos. A month ago, it worked. Archie Jefferson was the chief recruiter."

"Archie's involved with Danny Parva too?" asked Gemma.

"He's been in that gang since he was a teenager. Later he worked in deep cover as a college kid, even though he never bothered to go to college."

"Wait a minute," said Gemma, hearing even more than that. "You said three months ago they started recruiting Dommi. Which means this all started when Archie raped me?"

Mick stared at Gemma with sympathy in his eyes. "I didn't know it at the time, but yes, Gemma. That's when it started."

"And Dommi knew?"

"About what Archie had done to you?" asked Mick. "No. Dom didn't know anything about what that bastard did. They were recruiting him about the same time that happened to you, but Dom didn't succumb to their interest in him until a month ago."

"No way Dom would have gone for that," said Reno. "No way."

"What about Judge Hawkins and those sorority sisters?" asked Sal. "Did they have something to do with this too?"

"Those sorority sisters were paid by a person they thought wanted Gemma to be the keynote speaker at the sorority's next event. They were paid to fly to Vegas, call Gemma out of the blue and get her to meet them at Gateshead bar.

"At Clyde's place," said Reno.

"Right," said Mick. "They assumed she would mention it to Sal and he'd show up under cover, just to keep an eye on them since they called her out of the blue. And he did show up."

"But I didn't mention it to him," said Gemma. "Curtis mentioned it to him."

"But he showed up. And Hawkins showed up berating you, knowing Sal would have to handle that."

"That cop Hawkins showed up with was fake?" asked Sal.

"Yes," said Mick. "They knew you would have to approach him later, at his place, because of that cop's presence. Then they set up the kidnapping to take place in the parking garage at Hawkins' condo."

"I'll be damn," said Sal.

Trina frowned. "But wait a minute. Mick, you said this Parva person runs an assassin group. Are you telling us that our son goes around killing people just for money?"

Mick didn't respond. That was exactly what he was telling her.

"But he does it in service to his country like Trevor Reese," said Trina. "Right?"

"Or does he do it in service to the highest bidder?" asked Sal.

Mick didn't want to admit it. "To the highest bidder," he said.

Trina and Reno both were shaking their heads. "That's not true," said Trina.

"That's bullshit," said Reno. "I know Danny Parva. I know what kind of outfit he runs. But to say Dommi's mixed up with those bastards? That Dommi let them recruit him as a hired gun? Our son wouldn't do that shit."

"He did it and he's doing it," said Mick firmly, his hard green eyes staring at Reno. "Sal was his first assignment."

Sal frowned. "I was his first assignment? What was the assignment? What are you talking, Uncle Mick?"

But Gemma understood immediately. "Good Lord," she said. "Hired guns? Are you saying they targeted Sal for *assassination*?"

"That's what he's saying," said Nikki. "That's what that kidnapping was about."

264

Reno's heart was hammering. "Are you telling me this Parva gang ordered Dom to take Sal out?"

"Yes," said Mick.

"Then why the fuck is Sal still here," said Reno, "if that was the plan? Dommi came to his senses and refused to obey that order?"

"No," said Mick. "He obeyed it."

Now all of the Gabrinis were confused. "With all due respect, Uncle Mick," said Reno, "but your ass talking crazy now. What the fuck you mean he obeyed it?"

Mick leaned forward, which worried the heck out of all of them. "I've got a snitch doing time in prison alongside Danny Parva. I asked Hammer Reese to set it up so that my guy could become Danny's roommate."

"So what?" asked Reno. "You seem to have a guy everywhere."

"Parva told my guy that Dominic fired several rounds into Sal. He told him that Dom killed Sal. He also told my guy that unbeknownst to Dommi, they supplied him with fake bullets."

"What do you mean fake bullets?" asked Sal.

"That was why you had all of that residue and blood on your body, Sal," said Reno. "They used those blood and guts bullets."

Gemma frowned. "What are blood and guts bullets?"

"They're fake. Make it look like you're bleeding and have a bullet hole or whatever through your chest. Those bullets cause that residue we saw on Sal."

"Why didn't you say so when we saw it on Sal?"

"Because how was I to know that's what that was? I didn't realize it until Uncle Mick said the gun had fake bullets."

"But I still don't get it," said Sal. "Why wouldn't they want to take me out if that was the plan?"

"Parva's not stupid. He wasn't about to take you out. He was testing Dom to see if he'd take you out. He needs a strong man to run his outfit while he's incarcerated. But that strong man can't have allegiances to us. He needed to see if Dom would go all the way."

"And he didn't," said Reno. "See, Sal. I told you Dommi wouldn't do that shit."

Sal frowned. "What are you talking he wouldn't do it? He did it! He didn't know those bullets were fake. Uncle Mick said so himself!"

"Bullshit! He did know."

"He didn't know, Reno, what's your problem? Dommi's a fuck-up and always will be."

"Sal don't," warned Gemma.

"No, he wants to go there, let's go there," Sal said, and then he looked at Reno again. "You always put all your eggs in Dommi's basket because he's Trina's son. But you never put Jimmy on that pedestal because he has a different mother."

"That's bullshit, Sal, and you know it," said Trina.

"No, it's not bullshit," said Sal defiantly. "No hell it's not!" He looked at Reno. "It's always Trina's children that comes first, and then there's Jimmy. Remember that time you allowed that asshole to shoot Jimmy just to save Dommi? Remember that shit, Reno? You've always put that asshole first. Now look where we are. How's Dommi working out for you now, Reno? How's Dommi's dumbass working out for you now?!"

Reno's control broke and he jumped on Sal. Both men fell to the floor wrestling each other to the death. Trina and Gemma were screaming at them and trying to pull them apart, and Nikki was trying with all she had to break it up too. But Mick didn't lift a finger.

"Let'em work it out," he finally ordered. "They need to work it out."

And although Nikki obeyed his order immediately, the two wives were too concerned for their husbands. They didn't give a damn about Mick's commands in that moment.

"Stop it both of you!" Gemma was yelling.

"Damn animals!" cried Trina.

But then they had no choice but to give up, too, as those two middle-aged men kept rolling around on that floor trying to best the other one. But neither one of them gave an inch. They were fighting to the death to a draw.

And they both realized it. And soon they were too tired to even get to the draw. It was a horrible situation and that was all there was to it.

Sal got up first. Then he reached down and gave Reno a hand up.

Then they all sat back down, and Mick was able to continue telling what he knew.

"It was Brick Brusconi who got the ball rolling."

Sal was puzzled. "Brick Brusconi? He

ran one of my affiliate organizations. What the fuck he had to do with Danny Parva's outfit?"

Mick looked at Nikki.

"Brick wanted to take over Monk Paletti's territory," Nikki explained. "He hired the Parva Group to take Monk Paletti out."

Sal was shocked. "Brick wanted to take Frankie Paletti out? Get the fuck out of here! Brick knew the Gabrinis and Sinatras have an alliance with Frankie Paletti."

"That didn't matter to Brick," said Mick. "He wanted The Monk's territory."

"But wait a minute," said Sal. "Brick's kid, Luke, told me on his dying bed that it was some other group that went after Frankie."

"Because that was what his old man was telling him," said Mick. "But his old man wanted The Monk's territory. Monk beat his ass back. Then he hired the Parva Group to take Monk out. That's when I took Brick and his entire organization out."

Sal was stunned. "That was you? You

took out Brick's organization? Why didn't you tell me and let me handle that?"

"Because your ass believes in second chances," said Mick. "My ass don't. I handled it for you."

"But what's all of this about?" asked Gemma.

Mick looked at her. "It's about you."

Gemma was shocked. "*Me*?"

Sal was shocked. "*Gemma*? Why would it be about my wife?"

"I've never even heard of Danny Parva," said Gemma.

"What beef he got with my wife?" asked Sal.

"I don't know any of that yet," said Mick. "Parva mentioned her name to my guy. He said he hated her, but that's all he said about it. But she was the only name he mentioned. And he only just mentioned that when Archie gave him the report about Dommi passing the test."

"Parva thinks I'm dead?"

"Parva, no," said Mick. "But Dommi? Yes."

This time Reno nor Trina disputed that fact. It was getting harder and harder for them to dispute the facts. But they still couldn't believe it.

"But even recruiting Dommi may be about getting to Gemma in some way. That maybe he figures if Dommi would take his own uncle out, then surely he'd take out his wife. I don't know," said Mick. "But there we are."

"Maybe Parva's related to one of your clients, Gem," said Trina. "Like Miss Bettye's son. What's his name? Isn't he biracial?"

"His name is Donte," said Gemma. "And, yes, he is biracial."

"We need to go to that prison and talk to Donte," said Trina. "He may know what's going on."

"My guys already talked to Donte," said Mick. "He admitted that his brother is caught up with the Parva Group, but they see no evidence that he is. Parva doesn't know Donte from Adam, from what my snitch told me. And he barely knows Archie. That's not the angle."

"Then what is?" asked Gemma.

But Sal already saw the angle. "We need to talk to Dommi."

Reno looked at Mick when he didn't object. "You know where our boy is?" he asked him.

Mick didn't respond.

"That's why you wanted the ladies with us. You want Trina to talk to Dom, don't you, Mick?"

"You know where he is?" Trina asked.

Mick still didn't respond.

"Take us to our child," Trina said with a plea in her voice. "Mick, *please.*" She was desperate now. Reno placed his arm around her.

Mick hesitated, then he stood up and began walking to his office again. They all followed him.

He pressed the button and opened his wall-sized coat/gun closet once more. Then he looked at them. "Arm yourselves," he said.

None of them had to be told twice. They began grabbing guns like the gangsters they were. Even Gemma was packing. But was it enough?

"Any suggestions on which ones we should take, Uncle Mick?" asked Reno. "I mean, you've got every motherfucking weapon known to man up in this bitch. You've got everything I've ever heard of. Since you're the only one who seems to know what we're getting ourselves into, which ones should we take?"

Mick looked at Reno as if he was digesting what he'd just said to him. Then he looked at his enormous gun closet. "Take everything," he said, and then he left the room.

The Gabrinis looked at each other. Was that motherfucker for real? Going to talk to Dommi would require all of this? Now they were really worried.

But they didn't delay. They armed themselves to the teeth.

CHAPTER TWENTY-FIVE

After nearly seven miles of driving, Mick drove his big, black Cadillac Escalade down the longest stretch of dirt road the Gabrinis had ever seen. Even Nikki had never traveled that road before. The only place that topped it for isolation, in her memory, was the Kirkland safe house where Teddy had the rest of the family holed up.

After what seemed like miles, Mick finally pulled over to the side of the road. Both sides of the road were surrounded by thick woods, and no lighting whatsoever even though it was nightfall. The headlights of their SUV was the only illumination. It was like the land that time forgot.

Mick turned to Nikki, who was seated beside him on the passenger seat. "You and the ladies will stay here."

"Yes, sir."

"You get behind this wheel. If you hear gunfire, I want you to make a sharp left and tear through these woods. Then you'll see a road. Travel that road until you see me. Understood?"

Nikki nodded, although the task he laid before her seemed impossible. Tear through *those* thick woods? There's a road back *there*? But she trusted her father-in-law with her life. He would never say it was so if it wasn't. "Yes, sir," she said.

The men, after ordering their wives to shoot anything moving, got out of the SUV along with Mick. They, too, wondered where the hell was he taking them.

But they followed him through those thick woods. Within seconds they realized there was a road back there. "Leave it to Mick the Tick," Sal whispered to Reno as they walked, "to find a hideout this off the grid."

"Mick the Tick my ass," replied Reno.

"Trapper John better be his name tonight."

Mick, walking ahead of them, smiled. But after walking several more feet, he stopped them. And then opened up another thicket of woods that they went through. And then, when he opened up yet another thicket, there was light. Plenty of it. And a small, shack of a house. And right there, in plain sight, were the two men they were looking for: Dommi and his partner in crime, Archie Jefferson. They were drinking bottled beer, working on an old broken-down Ford Mustang, and listening to rap music. What angered Reno and Sal was that they both were talking and laughing as if they didn't have a care in this world. As if they were on top of the world!

Sal, who was angry with both of them, couldn't take his eyes off of the good-looking Archie the Rapist. It was that punk-ass bitch he wanted to get his hands on first. He knew Reno would handle Dommi.

Mick saw their impatience too. And he

wasn't going to hold them back. "Just remember," he warned them, "we need them both alive. For intel. Understood?"

"I'll try my best not to kill that bastard, if that's what you mean," said Sal, unable to take his eyes off of the man who violated his sweet wife. "I'll try my best."

Mick knew Sal was reliable. And he knew Reno was going to kick his son's ass, but he wouldn't kill him either. At least not yet. So he nodded. "Go get'em, gentlemen," he said, and Sal and Reno took off through those woods like bats out of hell. And there was no doubt where each one was headed. Reno had Dommi in his crosshairs, and Sal had Archie.

As soon as both of the young men saw the Gabrini men running out of those woods and coming for them, they dropped that torque wrench and those pliers and took off, both going in different directions. Dommi ran around the right side of the shack house. Archie ran down the left side. Reno ran after his son. Sal ran after his foe. And the foot race was on.

It should have been no contest. Two middle-aged men running after two young men in their prime? But it was a contest. Because anger was driving Reno's feet, and hatred was driving Sal's. They were right on the tails of those now-terrified pricks.

Sal was especially fast. He was Sal the high school athlete again. He was Sal the crooked cop again. He was that bastard that didn't take shit from anybody again as he kept humping and humping through woods that were scratching his ass as he tore through them. But wherever Archie was going, he was following. It was judgement day for that bastard. He was going to pay for what he did to Gemma.

Archie was floored when he first saw Sal Gabrini. Dommi had killed that bastard. He saw him load those bullets in his body with his own two eyes. He saw that pool of blood. And now that same asshole was chasing him? How could that be? He couldn't even wrap his mind around that shit.

But Sal was gaining on him. He wrapped his mind around that shit! And that was why he pulled out his weapon and started firing on Sal.

Back on the main dirt road, Nikki heard that gunfire. Remembering what Mick ordered her to do, she was already behind the wheel of his Escalade.

"Go, Nikki! Go now, Nikki!" Both Trina and Gemma were urging her as if they had to beg her. But she was already on it. She slung that big tank-looking SUV toward the left and tore through those woods just as she was ordered. And as soon as she saw that road, she took off down it. Trina and Gemma had their weapons out and was ready for whatever. They were only praying that neither one of their men, nor Dommi's dumbass, were hurt.

Sal wasn't hurt by a long shot. There

were so many woods on either side that Sal was able to easily elude any gunshots Archie was firing his way, and to get a few rounds off himself.

Both men kept running until they ran out of real estate: a high fence in front of them. The younger man saw that fence as his salvation. He quickly hopped on that fence ready to climb over and get away from that ghost called Sal Gabrini.

But Sal hopped up on that fence, too, and was able to grab Archie by the back of his trousers just as he was about to make it over the fence. And although Archie was younger and faster, Sal was far stronger. And with that Herculean strength and that muscular body, Sal was able to grab Archie Jefferson's ass and pull that raping motherfucker all the way down to the ground.

And as soon as Archie fell onto his back, Sal was on top of him. Sal was straddling him and punching him so hard that every punch was breaking another bone in Archie's high-cheek-boned face.

"You raped *my wife*?" Sal kept yelling at him as he brutalized him. "*My wife*? You had the balls to rape *my wife*?"

Then his anger went to another level and all he saw was red. "Rape this, motherfucker!" he started screaming. "Rape this, motherfucker! Rape this!"

Archie was screaming in agony as Sal was killing him. And there was no way Sal could stop. He thought about the terror Gemma had to have felt on that day, and then to keep it to herself to protect that asshole's mother, and then to have the guilt in knowing this bastard was a part of that kidnapping. And all those months of pain she endured alone that could have destroyed their marriage. It was too much. Sal had no stopping sense and didn't want any either.

Until he felt that hard, cold hand of Mick Sinatra. He didn't even hear that Escalade drive up. Nikki had picked Mick up further back and then raced to where they heard the gunfire. And Mick had jumped out of the truck ahead of everybody else, and grabbed Sal by the shoulder.

But Sal was still flailing at air even as Mick had picked him up. And then he was kicking and stomping on Archie even after he was on his feet again. Gemma ran up and as soon as she saw Archie in the flesh again, her anger broke like Sal's and she started stomping on him too. Nikki and Trina had to run up and grab Gemma before she and Sal killed that fool.

"Put her in the truck," Mick ordered, and Nikki and Trina pulled Gemma into the SUV. Mick had to drag Sal away from Archie and put him in the truck. Then Mick grabbed up a nearly unconscious Archie and threw him in the very back of the SUV, away from the Gabrinis. He sat back there with Archie.

But Trina was still worried sick.

"Where's Reno?" she asked. "Where's Dommi?"

"Turn around Nikki," Mick ordered from the third row. "Reno took off after Dommi in a different direction."

Nikki turned that big tank around, and hurried away from that fence.

Reno was on the other side of the woods still chasing his own son. Dommi was fast, but Reno was keeping up. He wasn't right on his tail the way Sal had been with Archie, but he could still see him and was gaining ground rather than losing it.

But just as he was keeping pace with Dommi, the arm of Reno's suitcoat got snared on one of the thickets of branches in those woods, and a thorn pierced through to his arm, causing it to draw blood. Reno screamed out from the pain and the anger that he was stopped in his tracks by a fucking branch!

Dommi, who actually felt as if he was

getting away from his angry father, heard his father's scream. When he looked back and saw that he was stopped and screaming in pain, his heart dropped. And he didn't delay. He ran back to Reno to help him. That was still his father. And despite his choices, he still loved his father, and his family, to pieces.

Reno was shocked and pleased that his son came back to his aid. Because he desperately needed it. That thorn was still stabbing into his arm.

Reno's heart broke when his son was within an inch of him, and he could smell his scent and he could touch him again. He still couldn't believe Dommi would have done that to Sal. He still couldn't believe it! But he knew he had to.

That was why, as soon as Dommi was able to release him from that thorn, Reno didn't stumble or stutter. He grabbed his son and began to beat the shit out of him. Even with his bad, bleeding arm, he was beating on

Dommi with both fists.

Dommi was crying out, but it was too late for tears for Reno. This was his flesh and blood. This was his beloved boy gone astray. And from that day forward, if they didn't kill him, he was taking charge of Dommi. No longer Mick. No longer Sal. Reno was taking over.

And the first order of business was an ass whipping to end all ass whippings. And Dommi was feeling it already.

"How could you?" Reno kept crying as he beat his son. "How could you do that to family, Dominic? How could you!"

What saved him was his uncle's big, black Escalade. It drove up, Mick jumped out, and just like he had to do with Sal, he had to drag an angry Reno away from Dommi lest he killed him too.

While Mick was throwing Reno into the SUV, Nikki had gotten out and grabbed Dommi, who was under her command before he decided to jump ship, and threw him into the back of the SUV alongside his partner in crime.

When Trina saw the condition of her son, she hurried onto that third row. Dommi was looking at her with tears in his battered eyes, needing her to hold him. But Trina, *being Trina*, slapped the shit out of him first. That anger had to go somewhere. But then she pulled him into her arms and held him. Dommi cried like a baby. When she saw Archie turn his head toward her, she slapped the shit out of him too. For Gemma. "What your ass looking at?" she angrily said to him.

Nikki got back behind the wheel of the Escalade as Mick sat in the third row with Trina, alongside the two badly beaten, terrified hoodlums, and then Nikki sped them up out of there.

CHAPTER TWENTY-SIX

Inside one of the guest houses at the Sinatra compound, Mick, Nikki, and the Gabrinis sat in front of Dommi and Archie as if they were still trying to figure that shit out. Archie was barely alive. He was slumped over with both of his eyes swollen shut, and blood still trickling from various parts of his body, including his balls. Sal saw to that.

But Archie wasn't so far gone that he

couldn't keep taking peeps at that ghost called Sal Gabrini with the little vision he still had left.

Sal frowned. "What the fuck is your problem?" he finally asked him. "What the fuck you looking at?"

"How can you be alive?" asked Archie. It was as if that question mattered more to him than life itself, given the danger he was still in. But that was the question he asked.

"I saw Dommi kill you," he kept talking. "I saw it with my own two eyes. I saw it."

Reno looked at his son. "So it's true then? Your ass pulled that trigger?"

They all stared at Dommi. But Dommi was so frustrated and flustered that he just rolled his head around and said nothing.

Trina was staring at him too. "Why aren't you surprised like the rapist is surprised? Why aren't you weirded-out that your uncle Sal is still alive and well?"

They all continued to stare at Dommi, because Trina had a point. Never once did he seem surprised that Sal wasn't dead.

But his silence only angered Reno. He slapped Dommi upside his already aching head. "You heard your mother, boy! Why aren't you surprised?"

Dommi let out a hard exhale, and then he spoke. "Because I changed the gun," he said.

Even Mick was surprised by that answer. "You changed the gun?"

"The Parva Group has an ironclad rule that they never use their own weapons and they never use their own transportation on any job. When the driver of the getaway van handed me the gun to use to take out Uncle Sal, I acted like it was a piece of shit gun and threw it aside. And I used my own gun. I used my gun because I had already switched out the bullets to those fake-ass blood and guts bullets. There was no way I was gonna harm Uncle Sal."

The sigh of relief in that room was

palpable. Even Mick sighed relief. Reno and Trina went to their son. And although they were so happy they could hardly contain themselves, Dommi only remembered the ass whooping his father had put on him, and the slap that twirled his head around like *The Exorcise* that his mother had put on him. He flinched when they approached him. But when they hugged him, he cried like the reckless-ass baby they knew he still was.

Even Sal and Gemma were relieved. "Thank God," Sal said when Dommi told them what happened. "Thank God."

But Mick was already on his phone.

"Who are you calling?" Gemma asked him.

"Jonah Bark."

"Who's Jonah Bark?"

"The driver of that van."

Reno and Trina stopped hugging their son and everybody looked at Uncle Mick. "You know the driver?" asked Reno.

"Yes."

Reno frowned. "But how?"

"When Danny Parva told my snitch that he wanted to take out Sal but didn't want to use his own men, the snitch recommended somebody. Jonah Bark was the man he recommended."

"And Jonah Bark worked for you, Uncle Mick?" asked Dommi. He was in shock more than anybody else in that room.

Mick nodded. "Yes," he said. "I made certain the bullets were fake in the gun Dommi was supposed to use."

Reno smiled. "Are you telling me this Jonah character had blood and guts fake bullets in his gun that he gave to Dommi, just like Dommi had fake bullets too?"

Mick nodded. "That's what I'm telling you, yes."

Even Sal was smiling. "I was gonna be alright either way," he said. Then his smile left. "Although nobody knew what Dommi's ass was up to."

"But why are you calling Jonah Bark?" Gemma asked Mick.

"I trust but verify too," said Mick as Jonah came on the line. Mick placed the call on Speaker.

"Mr. Sinatra, hey."

"How did it go today?"

"It was handled, sir."

"No problems or glitches?"

There was a pause. Then an answer. "Yes, sir. I was gonna call you but . . . I was afraid that you'd blame me, sir, when it wasn't my doing."

"Blame you for what, Jonah?"

"You haven't recovered the body, sir? The driver of the Bugatti was supposed to park it in that alley by Sal's house. It's not there?"

"It was there," said Mick.

"I handed Dommi the gun to use, sir. I handed it to him just like he knew was the protocol. But Dommi's ass didn't use the gun.

He tossed it aside, called it a punk-ass gun or something. Before I could even react to what he was doing, he pulled out his own gun and started shooting Mr. Gabrini like the man was target practice for his ass. I was stunned, sir. But I couldn't do anything about it. Before I could blink an eye, it was already done. Dommi had already killed his own uncle. That boy's crazy."

"Or sly like a fox," said Mick, and Dommi smiled. Which prompted both Reno and Trina to slap him upside his head.

"Am I in trouble, sir?" Jonah asked.

Mick exhaled. "You should have phoned me as soon as it happened, Jonah."

"Yes, sir."

"You're not in trouble, no. But you will receive a visitor. You will be hospitalized in severe pain. But you'll live. Oh, and your ass is also fired," Mick added, and then ended the call.

But despite his parents' anger, Dommi

was relieved. "See? I told y'all I wouldn't harm Uncle Sal! I didn't know that driver gave me a gun with fake bullets. I didn't know none of that shit. But I knew I wasn't gonna ever in my lifetime hurt my uncle. Or anybody else in my family. I knew that."

Mick had long ago accepted that what Dommi did to Joey, who was his family too, was unavoidable. But that still didn't lessen the sting inside of Mick's heart whenever it was dredged back up.

"Why?" Mick asked Archie.

"Why what?" Dommi responded.

"I'm talking to Archie Jefferson."

Archie looked his swollen eyes at Mick.

"What's Parva's game? Why did he order you to rape Gemma Gabrini? Why did he specifically want her husband kidnapped as a test for Dommi? What's Parva's game?"

They all looked at Archie because those were questions they needed to know too.

"All I know," Archie responded, "is that

he wants her to suffer. That's why he ordered me to do what I did to her. He told me when my brother lost his appeal, which we all knew he would because he's guilty, that would be the time to do it. That's why he wanted her husband snatched. That's why they ambushed you guys when you got to Philly."

"They were trying to take Gemma out?"

"No," said Archie. "Parva doesn't want her taken out. That's why those IEDs weren't supposed to hit the SUV she was traveling in. Parva wants her to suffer. He wants her to not know why, and to suffer for a long, long time."

"But suffer for what?" asked a frustrated Sal. "What for?"

"I don't know what. He told me he wanted her to suffer, and that's all he said about it."

They all looked at Gemma. "It has to be one of your cases, Gem," said Trina. "A case they figured you should have won, but you lost. Why else would anybody want you to suffer?"

That was the conclusion of all of them, including Mick. Gemma was as straight-lace as any member of their family could get. It had to be related to her work as an attorney.

"What about that case Judge Hawkins was yapping on about in Gateshead?" asked Sal. "Could that be it?"

Gemma quickly shook his head. "No way. That kid killed his girlfriend and their unborn baby. She was hood and so was he. No Danny Parva would give a damn about either one of them."

"Did your firm have a hand in defending Danny Parva's case at all?" asked Reno.

Gemma was shaking her head again. "I've never heard of him before, and no case is accepted by my law firm without my approval."

"Think hard about your recent cases, babe," said Sal. "Trina's right. The answer has to be in one of your cases."

Gemma exhaled. "I did have a string of losses lately," she said. "Not the firm. But me personally. Over the last two months, I haven't won one single case."

"What cases were those?" Trina asked.

Gemma listed them, including Donte's.

Mick looked at Archie. Although he already knew the answer, he needed to hear it from the brother who was in the Parva organization. "Is your brother connected to Danny Parva in any way?" he asked.

Archie was shaking his head. "No. This ain't got nothing to do with my baby brother. All Parva knows about him is what I told him. And I told him he was guilty as sin."

"When your mother finds out about what you've been up to," said Gemma, "it will kill her."

Archie frowned. "I know that."

"But yet you did it anyway?"

Archie shook his head. "We all gotta die from something," he said.

That angered Gemma so much that she jumped up and with her high heel kicked him right in the face, knocking him over the chair he was sitting in. He started bleeding and screaming out in pain again.

Even Reno was impressed. "Well *damn,* Gemma! You ever considered professional kickboxing?"

Everybody laughed. But Gemma was thinking about sweet Miss Bettye. It was no laughing matter to her.

CHAPTER TWENTY-SEVEN

The safe house was called *Kirkland* because it was near Kirkland Street, although it was miles away from any street and isolated even more so than the shack Dommi and Archie were holed up in. It was well-fortified, well-guarded, and quiet as the night was long. The youngest kids and baby Teresa were asleep: Grace and Oprah were with them. The older kids were in the family room, either playing video games or, in the case of Sophia and Destiny, talking about their men. The older set, Tommy, Teddy, Jimmy, and Roz were at the dining room table playing cards. It was Tommy and Jimmy versus Teddy and Roz. Tommy and Jimmy were winning.

All was quiet, until Mick's youngest children Duke and Jackie came up front. They were twins and always seemed to run together.

Duke sat beside his mother. Jackie sat beside their Uncle Tommy. Like her father, Tommy was her favorite too. But unlike her father, her reason was entirely different. To Jackie, Tommy was the best-looking man she had ever laid eyes on in her entire life, and she had a monster crush on him.

"Where's everybody?" Roz asked the twins as she threw down a card.

"The younger kids are all asleep. Everybody else are in the back room playing video games or talking smack or watching TV."

"I'm surprised you're still here, Ma," said Jackie. "I thought you'd be gone by now. But you're still here."

"Not by choice," said Duke. "Daddy won't let her leave."

Teddy and Tommy laughed. Roz failed to see the humor. "I'm gonna kick Mick's ass when I get out of here."

"Sure, Roz," said Teddy. "Just like all those other times you kicked his ass, right?"

302

"I'm serious!"

"He gives you liberties, Ma," said Teddy. "I'll give you that. I've seen your ass slap Pop and he didn't so much as raise a hand to hit you back. But you still jump to his commands just like the rest of us. For real though."

"Ah fuck you, Teddy," Roz said with a smile, and they all laughed at that too.

But then suddenly they heard what sounded like a sonic boom it was so loud, and every one of them scrambled up from that table in panic, as Tommy, Teddy, and Jimmy grabbed their guns and ran up front to see what was happening.

"Get to the back," Roz ordered the twins. "Duke, put everybody in the same room!"

"Yes, ma'am," Duke said as he and his sister hurried toward the back.

But when Tommy, Teddy, and Jimmy looked out of the front window, they were shocked. Every one of their security people were on the ground dead, with the front gate blown off of its hinges, and what looked like over a hundred men descending on the safe house.

"Ma!" cried Duke from the back side of the house.

Roz, her gun out too, ran to her son. He was looking out of the back window. Roz ran up to the window and looked out too. The security people guarding the back of the safe house were all down and dead too, and another army of over a hundred men strong were descending on the safe house from the backside. Roz's heart dropped through her shoe. "Call your father," she ordered Duke.

CHAPTER TWENTY-EIGHT

When Mick looked at his phone and saw that his son was calling, he answered quickly. But he couldn't get a word in from the sound of gunfire and Duke's frantic voice.

"We're under attack, Daddy!" he cried. "We're under attack! There's . . ."

Mick and Nikki and the Gabrinis all jumped up in shock. "Duke?" Mick called out over the phone. "Duke?" But the line had already gone dead.

Mick began running out of that safe house like a man terrified. Not only were all of the Gabrinis in that house, but his twins were in that house, and Teddy. And Roz was in that house! *His Roz*! He couldn't get out of that house fast enough.

Reno and Trina grabbed up Dommi and they were running out too. Sal quickly pulled his weapon, Archie started begging for his life, but Sal didn't hesitate. He shot Archie through the head and the heart without batting an eye, and then he grabbed Gemma and they took off too. Gemma would have looked back at Archie. She knew she would have felt no remorse for that monster. But she was thinking about her baby in that safe house, and Lucky and Marie and all the other family members in that so-called safe house. She didn't give Archie a second thought. She just ran.

When she and Sal got outside, Mick was already barking out orders. "I want every man at Kirkland!" Mick was yelling to his grounds security as he ran to his SUV. "And anybody else who's not here, get them there!" he yelled and all of his men onsite began running to the other SUVs, too. They'd never seen the boss that animated.

But Mick didn't give a shit about animation. He had to get to his family! He and Nikki and the Gabrinis hopped into that Escalade and took off. Normally Nikki would have stayed with the crew to supervise. But Teddy was in that house, and their baby too. She was in no condition to supervise anybody. She just wanted to get there.

And Mick was determined to get them there in record time. He was flying through that gate. And nearly ten other SUVs loaded down with the compound security, all Escalades too, were flying right behind him.

Sal and Gemma and Reno and Trina were on their phones trying to reach each and every one of their family members. Everybody was calling everybody inside that safe house, but nobody was answering their phones. Not even Tommy. Not even Teddy! Everybody in that Escalade were stricken with fear.

And suddenly, just as Mick was about to try his wife's phone again, a text came over his car screen. Mick quickly opened the text. It was a link to a video recording.

"What's that?" asked Nikki.

Mick didn't know. He pressed on the link. And they all saw for themselves that it was a live feed right inside of the safe house. The camera was scanning the massive-sized back room. Every family member was in that room, sitting down, with a small army of men standing over them with guns on them. Every member of that family, including Tommy and Teddy, looked terrified. Even baby Teresa, in Grace's arms, was at gunpoint too.

One man none of them had ever seen before, an older man with a patch over one of his eyes, came onto the screen and was talking directly into the camera. "Lest you think this is all we have," he said with a heavy accent Mick recognized as Hungarian, "I am going to go outside and show you the breath of us." He then, with the camera following him, went outside of the safe house and the camera panned around to show what looked like a full-scale army of men around the front of the house, and the back. And all of Mick's men, all of them, were obviously dead.

"Good Lord," cried Gemma.

Then the man Mick inwardly decided to refer to as Eye Patch to remember that face, went back inside of the house and back into the room where everybody were housed. "Now you listen and you listen good," Eye Patch said into the camera. "You are not to come anywhere near this house. We have a helicopter on you right now. You and your men pull over to the side of the road and wait my further instructions. If you do not do so," Eye Patch said, "then this will happen every second you don't." And he turned, aimed his gun specifically at Roz, and immediately shot her in the arm to the horror of everybody in the house, and in the Escalade too. Mick nearly wrecked his SUV, and had to swerve to get back on the road, when he saw his wife getting shot. "Lord no," he was mumbling. "Lord no."

"Pull over, Mick!" Sal cried out, seeing the state he was in. "Pull over before that bastard shoots somebody else!"

Mick quickly pulled over to the side of the road. The ten SUVs behind him, who didn't know what was going on, followed his lead and pulled over too.

Roz had grabbed her arm and was slumped over in pain as all of the family in that room hurried to her aid. But it was Tommy who took charge and quickly began wrapping her injury, to staunch the flow of blood.

Mick knew he had to keep his cool. He knew he had to find out all the intel he could find out before he could have any plan of attack. Nikki, too, knew she had to keep her wits about her as she hopped out of the Escalade to alert the lead SUV on what was going on, and for the lead to pass the word to the other SUVs. They wanted nobody going rogue in a situation like this.

"Who are you?" Mick asked as he stared at the man with the patch over his eye.

"It matters not a twit who I am. I am not your problem. Who I am does not get you from point A to point B. It gets you nowhere. I'm the man on the moon, if that makes you feel better. I'm the bogey man under your bed. I'm whatever you want me to be. Who I am matters not. What matters is what I want."

Mick knew it would come to that. And he steeled himself. "What do you want?" Mick asked as Nikki got back into the Escalade.

"I want Gemma Jones," said Eye Patch and Sal's heart dropped. He was about to yell out *no fucking way*, but Reno surreptitiously grabbed him by the arm. It was enough to stop Sal from saying a word.

Mick had already suspected it was Gemma they were after. But he needed more intel! "Why Gemma Jones?" he asked.

"Oh she knows why. That question is better asked of her. Isn't it, Miss Lady G? Isn't it?"

Gemma was mortified. She had no idea why they would want her. And an army of people there to get her? It made no sense!

"What are you talking about?" a distressed Gemma leaned forward from the second row and asked Eye Patch before Sal could stop her. "Is it one of the cases I lost? Just tell me which case!"

The man smiled. "Now you're on to something."

"But which case are you talking about? Which case did I lose that whomever you work for would be so angry about?"

"You're warm," said Eye Patch, "but not there yet."

But then Carmine, *being Carmine*, spoke up. "Aunt Gemma, it may not be a case you lost," he yelled out, "but a case you won!"

Reno and Trina's hearts dropped

through their shoes. Dommi's heart did too. And all three of them yelled out to that foolish child. "Carmine, shut the fuck up!" all three of them yelled at the same time. They were terrified that Eye Patch would shoot Carmine next.

But Eye Patch laughed. Which let Mick and everybody else in that Escalade know that Carmine had apparently hit the nail on the head.

"I am sending a team to where you are," said Eye Patch. "They will retrieve Gemma Jones, bring her to me, and then me and my army will leave this house with nobody else harmed. But remember: If you don't relinquish her to my team, then we will leave this house alright. But every single one of these people in this house will be killed. From the youngest," he said as the camera moved over to little Teresa, "to the oldest." The camera then moved over to Roz. "Don't fuck with me," he said, and then the camera went to black.

Sal grabbed Gemma as she began shaking in fear.

Even Mick was thrown. "Dear Lord," he said, which they all knew meant even to him it wasn't just horrific, but was DEFCON five hundred horrific!

"Who are they?" asked a worried Reno. "They can't all be Danny Parva's people."

"Parva's a very rich man," said Sal. "Killing people is a lucrative trade. And his ass in prison for the rest of his life. What he gonna do with that kind of dough in prison? He's got money to burn."

"But he ain't got this many men under his command."

"Those aren't his men," said Mick. "Those are mercenaries from Europe. They probably never saw Parva a day in their lives. He's just the man that's going to pay them when they finish the job. They probably never heard of me before either. Or they would have never touched my wife." Mick's jaw tightened

314

when he made that declaration. But he wasn't lying. And everybody in the SUV knew it too.

"Let's just go to that safe house and fight this shit out," said Reno.

"The man said they have a helicopter on us, Reno," said Trina. "They'll see us coming a mile away, you moron!"

"What you getting angry at me for?" Reno shot back. "I didn't do this shit!"

"We got to figure this out," said Sal, "because no way are they taking Gemma. No way."

"What do you mean no way?" asked a now angry Gemma. "Our baby is in that house, Sal! Our children and the rest of the family. I have to go!"

"No hell you're not!" declared Sal. "I'm going. They'll have to take me if they're taking anybody."

But Gemma wasn't thinking about him. When those men arrived, she had to go. She knew it, Mick knew it, everybody in that

Escalade knew it except for Sal. But Sal, deep down, knew it too.

"What case could he be talking about, Aunt Gem?" asked Nikki.

Gemma was shaking her head. "I don't know. If I only knew," she added distressingly as she tried with all she had to find something in the rolodex of her mind that she could draw on. "I haven't won a case in months!"

"What was the last one you won?" Nikki asked.

Gemma had to think about that one too. "It was a simple assault case. A young lady."

Sal was shaking his head. "That can't be it," he said. Then he began hitting his forehead with three of his fingers. "They're on their way to get her. We've got to come up with something. We've got . . ." And he fell back into his own thoughts.

"But why would somebody be angry with you," said Trina, "if you won the case?"

"Maybe it depends on who she won the

case against," said Nikki.

And suddenly it hit Gemma. "That has to be it," she said.

"What has to be it?" asked Sal.

And then it opened up for her. "That's it! He's the only one who called me that."

"Who's the only one that called you what?" asked Mick. Even he was looking anxiously at her through his rearview mirror.

Gemma looked at Mick. "Olsen."

Mick sat at attention. They finally had a name. "Olsen?" he asked.

"The guy with the patch called me Miss Lady G," said Gemma. "That's what one of my clients used to always call me when I was his lawyer. Miss Lady G. But I defended him years ago."

"What was the case?" asked Nikki.

Gemma had to think about that too. "He was accused of killing an auto mechanic in Spring Valley. But that case was years ago."

"What was the auto mechanic's name?"

asked Sal.

"Oh gosh," Gemma said, searching her brain. "It was a . . . a Jeb somebody."

"And the client was Olsen?" Mick asked.

"Yes." Gemma was certain now. "My client's name was Carl Olsen."

"And you got him off?" asked Reno.

"He was found not guilty on all counts, including first degree murder of that auto mechanic."

But Sal was looking at Mick. "You know him, Uncle Mick, don't you? Is he related to Danny Parva?"

Mick exhaled. "No. But a few months ago, when Parva got locked up, he found out who actually gunned down his old man. It happened a long time ago. The name Carl Olsen kept coming up and a lot of talk about how he got off on a murder charge that would have locked him up for life, and then the that same night he was set free he iced Parva's old man."

"Which means he's thinking his old man would still be alive had Olsen not been exonerated," said Trina.

Mick nodded. "Right."

"And since Gemma is the lawyer who got Olsen his freedom," added Trina, "she got in his crosshairs."

"Parva just found out about all of this when he got locked up. They didn't know who killed his old man all those years ago. And since his old man was a drug dealer, the cops didn't care either."

"But why go after Gemma?" asked Sal. "Why didn't he just go after Olsen?"

"Olsen's dead. Was shot and killed during a bank robbery a couple years back. Gemma and our justice system are all he's got left to blame. And since he can't go after the justice system for not finding his old man's killer and bringing him to justice, Gemma's all he's got."

"And he's going all-in on her ass," said

Reno.

"Right," said Mick.

"Oh, Lord," said Trina. "This isn't good."

"What are we gonna do now, Pop?" Nikki asked him. "Those people One-Eye said is on their way will be here soon." One-Eye was Nikki's name for the mercenary ringleader. "What are we going to do?"

But Sal had been thinking about that. "We're going to do the only thing we can do," he said, and everybody looked at him. "We're going to turn Gemma over to them."

"What?" asked Trina. "Have you lost your mind, Sal?"

"Keep going, Sal," said Gemma. "We gotta do something!"

"We're going to let you go with them," said Sal, "and myself, Uncle Mick, and Reno are going to get busy. We're going to make full use of the very reason why Uncle Mick always uses his own fleet of Escalades."

Everybody looked at him confused. But

Mick wasn't. "You got a plan, Salvatore?" he asked.

Sal nodded, although they all could tell it wasn't a plan he wanted to execute. But he knew he had no choice. For everybody's sake.

Then he looked at Gemma. A look of fear and distress was all over his tortured face. "You trust me, right? Don't you, Gemma?"

Gemma was nodding. "Yes, Sal."

"And I don't want you to worry, okay?"

"Okay."

"Don't worry, honey." He was rubbing her arm. This "plan" was killing him.

"Just tell us, Sal. I'll be okay. Just tell us the plan."

"It's the only way I can see where we can get out of this. But you'll have to go with them. They're mercenaries. They're paid to do a job. They won't harm you until they at least get you to that safe house."

Gemma was terrified, too, but she was nodding her head. She'd already concluded

321

herself that she had to go with them.

"We just got to make sure we handle our business before they get you to that safe house," said Sal.

"But that makes no sense," said Trina. "How are they not going to get her to that safe house before we can do something?"

"Let us worry about that," said Reno, but it still made no sense to Trina. How in hell were they going to stop an army?

"Uncle Mick?"

Mick looked at Sal.

"Get on the horn and tell the driver in the SUV directly behind us to pull up until it bumps our bumper, and then have him tell every SUV behind yours to do the same."

Mick didn't question it. He did as Sal told him to.

"And now what?" asked Reno when Mick got off of the walkie talkie function on his phone where all of his drivers could hear him at once.

"Get in Mick's seat, Nikki," Sal ordered, "and Mick you come back here and get us out of here."

That was confusing even to Gemma, but not to Mick nor Reno. Mick climbed out of his seat, Nikki got behind the steering wheel, and Mick made his way toward the back.

But when he got to Gemma he stopped. "Gem?"

"Yes, sir?"

"When those assholes get here, I want you to get out right away, okay? Don't wait for them to come to you. You get out and start heading to them."

"Okay."

"Sal's right. They're mercenaries. Their mission is to retrieve you and get back to base. They can't see shit in here with the tint on my windows, but I don't want them snooping. I don't want them asking questions."

"Yes, sir."

Then he looked at Trina. "While we're

gone, Katrina, you be the muscle, if any is needed." Then Mick frowned. "Given the numbers," he added, "let's pray none is needed."

Trina nodded. "Got cha, Mick."

"Don't try to be no fucking hero, Tree," Reno warned her. "I mean that shit!"

"I won't, Reno." Although everybody in that truck knew she would do whatever it took.

"And Dommi?" Reno said.

"Sir?" Dommi was so badly beaten that he was in no condition to do anything anyway.

"Your ass stay right where it is. I don't care if this motherfucker is under attack, you stay right there and take it. You hear me? I dare you to try that rogue shit this time."

"I won't, Pop. Just go save the family."

"Now he's worried about the family," said Reno. "Fuck you!"

Mick then moved to the third row where Dommi was seated and pressed a hidden button. The center of the third row began opening. Gemma and Trina, and even Dommi were amazed.

"Okay, let's go," said Sal to Mick and Reno, and then all three men went through that latch that placed them beneath the Escalade, and then the latch closed back shut.

Before they moved on, Sal looked from beneath the SUV and was able to see that chopper Eye Patch mentioned would be hovering above Mick's long row of SUVs. Then, as the women waited for the mercenaries to arrive, Mick, Reno, and Sal began crawling their way beneath every one of those ten other Escalades that were behind the lead Escalade, certain that the chopper in the area could not see them, until they made it to the last SUV, which was all the way around the corner because the line of SUVs were so long.

But for Sal, that was the good news.

"We need to get in this last one, Uncle Mick," said Sal and then Mick got on his phone and warned the driver of the last SUV that he was coming onboard from beneath.

One of the capos inside the last SUV pressed the button on the third-row flooring and the latch opened. He and the other capos onboard helped Mick, Sal, and Reno get onboard.

"Now what?" asked Reno to Sal when they got inside of the last SUV, a white Escalade.

"Get behind the wheel, Uncle Mick," said Sal. "You know how to work this fucker."

The three powerful men made their way up front and the capos upfront quickly gave up their seats and moved to the back of the SUV. Mick got behind the steering wheel and Sal got on the passenger seat.

"Get on the horn," Sal said to Mick, "and tell your guys that on your order you want SUV numbers three and four to fall out of formation until you tell them to fall back in line."

Reno frowned. "Why?"

But Mick did as he was told. He wasn't

able to come up with shit. Sal Luca at least had a plan. A plan Mick knew he wouldn't risk Gemma's life unless he was convinced they could pull it off.

Then Sal looked out of the panoramic sunroof above their heads and could see that the chopper was still hovering outside. Satisfied, he looked at Mick. "Tell them to drop out of formation now," he said, "and as soon as I give the word, I want you to floor this motherfucker and back it up all the way until you turn another corner. We got to get out of the sight of that chopper."

Mick understood what Sal was trying to do now. And he got on his phone's walkie talkie function and gave the order.

As soon as he did, SUV numbers three and four drove slightly out of formation.

Sal kept looking up through the sunroof, and as soon as he saw the chopper hover over numbers three and four to see what they were up to, he looked at Mick. "Now Uncle Mick!" he yelled.

And Mick quickly hit the gas petal and backed the white Escalade all the way back so fast that Sal and Reno thought they were on one of those dreaded rollercoasters.

"Don't kill us, Mick, damn!" decried Reno.

But Mick went even faster backing up that SUV. Until he turned another corner and rendered that SUV completely out of view of the chopper. And then he turned around and took off, and ordered the two SUVs to fall back in formation.

"Gotdamn, Sal!" Reno said excitedly. "You did that shit! You got us out of there. Now we can handle business at the safe house."

"Yeah, but two armies are waiting for us at that safe house," said a still-worried Sal. "We've got to handle business before they bring Gemma there."

"How the fuck we gonna do that?" asked

Reno.

But now that Sal got them out of the watchful eye of that chopper, Mick took over. As he drove the miles and miles to that safe house, he was on his phone the entire time, barking out all kinds of orders. He even contacted his lead field capo. "Don't go to the safe house," he ordered, in direct contradiction to his original order. "Here's what I want you to do instead."

CHAPTER TWENTY-NINE

By the time Mick, Sal and Reno had driven to the backside of the safe house, two streets over, the mercenaries were just driving up to the lead Escalade. Gemma did as she was told and got out as soon as they drove up. With the mercenaries jumping out with guns drawn, and the chopper overhead, she raised her hands and slowly walked toward them.

Nikki and Trina looked on in horror. "Sal's ass is mine if anything happens to Gemma."

"It won't," said Nikki. "He won't put his wife in harm's way unless he's certain he could

330

get her back in one piece. Boss wouldn't go for it either."

"Boss? You mean Mick? You sure about that? What's to say his ass just wanna get up in that safe house cause Roz up in there, and Gemma be damned?"

"His wife did get shot," said Nikki. "I'm sure he's worried sick about her. But at least he and Uncle Sal and Uncle Reno are giving everybody in that safe house a chance. That's more than any of them had before.   Boss knows what he's doing."

Trina stared at Nikki. She was acting like she was on Mick's band wagon just as much as he was on hers. She only prayed Nikki, who worked with Mick all the time, was right, as she watched Gemma get into that van and then the mercenaries hopped in too, and drove away.

"What are we waiting for, Uncle Mick?" Sal asked anxiously. "We gotta do this before they get here with Gemma. What are we waiting on?"

"Cover," said Mick.

"What cover?" asked Reno.

Then they began to hear what sounded like an army of choppers in the air. "That cover," said Mick.

They all knew Mick had a fleet of helicopters too, but they never dreamed he could have summoned them that fast. But he had.

Mick looked at his capos inside the SUV with them. "Wait until the choppers do what they do, and then I want you to do clean up. Make sure nobody cut down is still breathing. We'll take care of the inside."

The capos voiced their understanding and then Mick, Sal, and Reno got out.

They began walking swiftly toward the backside of the safe house and down a narrow pathway of abandoned houses, all of which Mick owned. It was the very reason he placed his safest safe house there: total and complete isolation. So far away from anybody else that it was off the radar of everybody else. And it was badly breached. Mick had course corrections to do!

But then he stopped walking and stopped Reno and Sal's progression too. Then he pulled out his phone and pressed the walkie talkie function again. "Everybody in place?"

"Yes, sir."

"Go now and go hard. Exterior only."

"Yes, sir."

Then Mick's phone rang. It was Nikki. He answered quickly. "They got her?"

"She's in the van, yes, sir."

"Which one?"

"The first one. All of the vans are white, but the one Aunt Gemma is in has a picture of a bald eagle on back. The only van in that convoy that has anything on it."

"Order the nine other SUVs to follow your lead. You guys stay with that van, but you don't want to cause a shootout. Stay at a safe distance."

"Yes, sir."

And as soon as Mick ended that call, Reno and Sal saw a long line of helicopters flying overhead at the safe house. And as soon as the choppers appeared, they were dropping IEDs on the army of mercenaries in the front and back of the safe house, taking them out *en masse*.

"Get ready," Mick said, his weapon raised. Reno and Sal got ready too.

As they did, some of the mercenaries from around back began running for cover down the path where Mick and the Gabrinis were, and they spared not one. They shocked them all and then shot them all as they appeared. Then Mick was on his walkie talkie again. "Let me know when it's all clear," said Mick.

"Yes, sir."

"What about the chopper helping

Gemma?" asked Sal. "Are they getting any cover over there to help her?"

"They'll take care of that location as soon as they clear this location."

"Why can't they do both?" Reno asked.

"Because they need that element of surprise, Reno," said Mick. "If they started dropping grenades over by the ladies, then the safe house would have been alerted. And that one-eye fool could have been dropping bodies inside my safe house. They had to have that element of surprise."

And then the call came in. "All clear, sir," the lead pilot said.

"Send a crew over to the van to take out that chopper following our guys," said Mick. "Then take out those vans heading this way. But don't touch the first van. It has a bald eagle on the back of it. The only one of the vans with a marking. That van you do not touch. Mrs. Gabrini is in that van."

"Yes, sir. We're on it."

And then Mick ended the conversation and he, Sal, and Reno took off.

Since they were on Mick's turf, they let him lead the way. And he led them up to the safe house where bodies littered the front and back. He led them through a side entrance that Reno and Sal had assumed was just the side of the house. But nothing was simple with Mick.

Inside the safe house, Eye Patch heard the attack outside and ordered a group of his men to go out and assist. He wasn't terribly worried because he knew they had the numbers. They were well-equipped to beat back any foe.

But by the time Mick, Sal, and Reno had entered the home through the unknown passageway, Eye Patch was beginning to panic. All of the men he were sending out to help were being gunned down by an aerial assault. And Eye Patch was frantically calling

Mick.

Mick kept walking down the corridor and answered the call on the first ring. "Yes?"

"What bullshit are you pulling?" Eye Patch screamed. "I'll start mowing down every motherfucker in this house if you don't call off those dogs and call them off right now! Are you out of your fucking mind? Do you wanna die?!"

"Do you?" asked Mick.

"I have a gun to your wife's head," Eye Patch was yelling. "I'll blow her brains out right in this room if you don't call off the hounds, I mean every word I speak to you. I mean every word! I will kill this bitch!"

"I dare you," said Mick.

And as soon as he said it, Mick, Sal, and Reno were at the door of the massive room where the family was located. By the time those mercenaries guarding the family saw them, they were already being gunned down.

"Everybody get down!" Teddy yelled as he and Tommy started firing on the mercenaries too. And everybody got down.

It all happened so fast that the mercenaries didn't have a chance to even lift up their weapons. They dropped like flies. But every Gabrini and Sinatra firing knew to keep one alive: preferably the leader.

And since Eye Patch was a coward in the long run, Sal noticed, it was an easy call. Because he might have only had one eye, but even he saw just how badly he had underestimated his opponent. He immediately surrendered. He dropped his gun to the floor and got on his knees like the punk he was.

Tommy kept his gun trained on him as Mick hurried over to his wife.

"Oh Mick!" Roz cried out, reaching out her arms to him. She was feisty with him when she didn't want to be at that safe house, but now she was behaving as if she had never been happier to see him in all her life. She was even kissing on him like he was some rock star. "I thought we all were gonna die," she admitted. "I thought there was nothing that could be done."

"How badly are you hurt?" Mick asked her, looking at her bandaged arm.

"Not bad. The bullet just grazed me I think. But it still hurts like hell."

Mick ordered his son Duke to phone their family doctor, who knew about Kirkland and knew how to be discreet. "Tell him to get here now."

"Yes, sir," Duke said as he got on the phone.

"Where's Nikki?" asked Teddy. "Is Nikki safe?"

Reno and Sal glanced at each other. Reno was pleased that his brood was okay, but Trina was still in harm's way. And after Sal saw that baby Teresa, still in Grace's arms, and Lucky and Marie were all okay too, and everybody else, he knew he had to act too. He looked at Mick. "I need a chopper and I need one now."

Mick didn't delay. He got on his phone and made the order. "Bring a chopper down now," he ordered, still holding Roz. "Sal Gabrini needs transport."

"Yes, sir."

"Dad, where's Mom?" Lucky was asking Sal. "Is Mom okay?" But Sal, Reno, and Teddy had already rushed out of the room.

Marie, concerned too, went over and hugged her baby brother. "She's okay," she said. "Don't worry, Lucci. Daddy's gonna make sure Mom is just fine."

Lucky hugged his sister back. But he was worried sick.

Mick saw it, too, and went over and gave Lucky a pat on the back. He was a good kid. But his main focus was Eye Patch. He walked over to him. Tommy still had his gun trained on that asshole.

"Tommy, take everybody out of this

room."

Tommy knew what that meant. "Sure thing, Uncle Mick," he said, still staring at Eye Patch and wishing he could get a round of licks in on that bastard himself for the terror he rained down on the family. But he did as he was told and moved the entire family out of the room. He closed the door behind them. It was just Mick and Eye Patch.

Mick wanted to make sure his theories were correct. "Who are you working for?"

Eye Patch viewed himself as a prisoner of war. But he wasn't holding anything back. "A Mr. Parva is all I know."

"Why Gemma Gabrini?"

"Gemma Jones is the name given to me. And the only information I have on that is that she's an attorney who got a man off of a murder conviction and then the same night that same man went out and killed Mr. Parva's father. Had she not gotten the killer off, he feels his father would still be alive today."

341

"His father was killed years ago. Why now?"

"He only just found out who his father's killer actually was, is my understanding. But unfortunately that man, the killer, is dead. But the woman who got him off and put him in position to kill Mr. Parva's father is still alive. He wanted us to bring her in, torture her, but keep her alive. He wanted her to suffer."

"Suffer like how?" asked Mick as he pulled out his gun and shot Eye Patch in the arm. "Like this? Like the way you shot my wife?"

Eye Patch grabbed his arm, as if he was surprised that Mick would harm him.

But his "harm" was just beginning. "Like the way you wanted my wife to suffer?" Mick asked. "Or like this?" Mick said, shooting Eye Patch in the leg, causing him to fall. "Or maybe like this?" Mick shot him again, this time in the other arm. Eye Patch was screaming out in pain now. But Mick kept on shooting him with bullets that grazed rather than penetrated. He wanted him to suffer too. And he was suffering. He was wrenching in pain.

"Nobody touches my wife," said Mick. "Nobody!"

Then he administered the fatal shot, and all of Eye Patch's screams went silent.

Then he thought about Nikki, whom he loved like his own child, and could only hope that she and Trina and Gemma would make it out of harm's way too.

CHAPTER THIRTY

By the time the chopper carrying Sal, Reno, and Teddy arrived on scene, all of the mercenary vans had been destroyed by Mick's choppers. Including the mercenary chopper, which was shot down. But the van with the bald eagle on back, the van carrying Gemma, was getting away.

Nikki and the nine other SUVs were in hot pursuit, but they weren't catching up. And the choppers in the air couldn't do anything, either, without endangering Mrs. Gabrini.

But Sal was furious. "Why are they letting them get away like this?" he demanded to know.

"What the fuck is wrong with them?" Reno was furious too.

"What could they do without risking Aunt Gemma?" asked Teddy. "Nikki knows what she's doing."

Teddy and Mick might have all that confidence in Nikki, but Sal's wife was the one in danger. Not Nikki. He looked at the pilot. "Hover over the van," he ordered, "and let me down."

"Down where, sir?"

"On top of the van."

"Uncle Sal!" said Teddy.

But Sal frowned. "What the fuck else can we do? You got a better idea?"

Teddy didn't. Sal thought so. "Hover over that van and let me down now," Sal ordered the pilot.

The pilot looked at Teddy. He was ultimately his boss. When Teddy nodded, he nodded too. "Yes, sir," he said, and flew in position.

Inside the van, all three mercenaries had their guns trained on Gemma. They were in panic mode after they witnessed all the other vans being destroyed by air assault. They knew they were only still alive because they had Gemma Jones onboard. They were also desperately trying to get a call in to the safe house, so that they could get some backup on the road, but nobody was picking up.

Then they heard a thump sound on the roof of the van. "What's that?" asked the youngest one.

"Somebody's on the roof," said the older one. "We got company!"

The two oldest grabbed up their guns and hurried to the door. They knew the sooner they acted, the more they could spook whomever was on top of their van. They quickly took their rifles and busted out both of the side windows, and then they quickly leaned out, with their guns trained toward the top of the van.

But Sal and Teddy, who were on top, weren't near the windows. They were purposely further over because they were expecting the mercenaries to come at them from the windows. And as soon as they saw those rifles sticking out, Sal on one side grabbed one gun, Teddy on the other side grabbed the other gun, and then they pulled the mercenaries out of the window and shot them both as they threw them, and their rifles, from the van. Both men rolled and rolled until they rolled into a ditch. Presumed dead on the spot.

The third mercenary, the youngest one, immediately tried to grab Gemma and put his gun to her head, for his own protection, but she was already on it. And as soon as she saw the other two men get thrown from the van, she kicked the younger man in his groin with her high heel and then she wrestled for control of his rifle. He was working on half-strength, given the pain he was in, but he was still younger and stronger than Gemma. But she wouldn't let go of that rifle. She was trying to buy time.

And it worked. Sal and Teddy flew in from the shattered windows and Sal was able to easily snatch the rifle away from both of them. Then he took that same rifle, shot that young mercenary, and threw him and his rifle from the van too.

While that was happening, Reno had leaned over the front end of the van from the rooftop and even with his banged-up arm he was able to bust open the windshield with his shotgun. The driver swerved, trying to knock Reno off, and Reno nearly fell off, but he was able to recover and put that shotgun dead smack in the driver's face. "Don't fuck with me!" he yelled. "Stop this van and stop it now!"

And the driver, knowing that there was no use continuing, slammed on brakes. He nearly dislodged Reno, which Reno was certain was what he was trying to do, but it didn't work. As soon as Reno got inside the van he removed the keys from the ignition, and then he took out the driver. Mick's SUVs, that had been witnessing the men and their rooftop escapades, finally caught up to the van. And Trina and Nikki hopped out and ran to their men. Dommi, fearful that his father would kick his ass again even as he was still feeling the pain from before, stayed put.

But Sal and Gemma were already together. They were hugging each other and kissing each other and happy that the ordeal was over. Even as they heard the police sirens in the distance, and they had loads of explaining to do, they didn't care. They were smiling for the first time in a long time.

"And here I was thinking my line of work was hazardous," said Sal. "Your lawyering ass is what got us in this jam."

Gemma grinned. And then they both laughed. But it wasn't the laughter of humor at all, but the laughter of great relief. It was over. Finally, it was all over.

EPILOGUE

Early Sunday morning and the streets of Paris were quiet. Sal and Gemma sat outdoors at a sidewalk café and watched the occasional car or person go by. They were good for nothing that day. Had been good for nothing their entire week in Paris, and they wouldn't have it any other way.

There were bodyguards all around them. Sal was still the second most powerful mob boss and was still worldwide. And Gemma was with him. He wasn't taking her protection for granted ever again. But his men knew how to stay out of sight so as not to constantly remind them that they weren't garden variety tourists the way they felt they were. This was their vacation, and nothing was going to stand in their way.

Sal crossed his legs. "I heard from Reno."

Gemma sipped her tea and looked over at Sal.

"He said Dommi's thrilled to be working for him in his casino."

Gemma laughed. "Reno's lying his head off."

"You know I know it," said Sal, smiling too.

"Unless Dommi is now co-owner of the PaLargio hotel and casino, which we know he is not," Gemma pointed out, "there's no way he's loving working anywhere but in gangster land. What job did Reno give him anyway? Entry level pit boss?"

"Not even," said Sal. "He's an assistant pit boss."

Gemma grinned. "Oh man! I know Dommi's pissed. I bet he's begging to get back with Uncle Mick. Or even with you."

"Reno got real and admitted as much. But he says that life is over for Dom. There's no going back for him anymore. Mick don't want him and I know I don't want his ass either, and Reno's not letting him go anyway. I say his ass better be glad he's alive."

"I know that's right," agreed Gemma. "What about Roz? You heard from Uncle Mick yet?"

"I haven't. You know his ass don't answer no phone calls unless he feels like it. Or if it's Tommy. But Tree spoke to Roz. She's doing great. Other than a scar on her arm, she has full function. Reno does too, with his arm."

"Good," said Gemma. "It all worked out." Then she looked at Sal. "Including Danny Parva, I assume."

Sal nodded. "Uncle Mick's guys took care of his ass. May he rest in turmoil."

But Gemma was shaking her head.

"Can you imagine? Somebody I defended so long ago, and completely forgot about, was the reason for all we went through. That's weird."

"But that's your profession," said Sal. "And we need to remember that from here on out. Your line of work ain't all that safe either."

Gemma already knew that. But she wasn't feeding into it because she knew Sal would take it to another level and insist on even more around-the-clock protection for her.

But then they heard the bells of St. Mary's. And they both relaxed again, and smiled.

"You know what?" asked Sal.

"What?"

"Let's forget all of that. Teresa' spending the next two weeks with Tommy and Grace. Lucky and Carmine are spending their summer with Big Daddy and his family. And Marie's thrilled to have the house all to herself. Our kids are doing great. And we've got another whole week in Paris. Let's think about that. It's a blessing, isn't it?"

"After what we've been through these past months and we're still standing? Nothing but a blessing."

"Then let's do it," Sal said as he unfolded his legs and stood up. He reached out his hand to Gemma.

Gemma looked up at him. "Let's do what?"

"Let's go to Mass. The cathedral is right around the corner. I haven't been in ages. I don't want this hot streak to end."

Gemma smiled. Leave to Sal to talk about church using a gambling reference! But she placed her hand in his hand and stood up too. "My man wants to go to worship? I'm for it. I'm for that all day long."

Sal smiled. Placed her arm on his arm. And then they walked down the cobblestone streets slowly and happily, like two young lovers on a brisk Sunday morning. Like they were and had always been footloose and fancy free. If only for a day.

Go to

www.mallorymonroebooks.com

or

www.austinbrookpublishing.com

or

www.amazon.com/author/mallorymonro

e

for more information on all titles.

ABOUT THE AUTHOR

Mallory Monroe is the bestselling author of over one hundred-and-fifty novels.
Visit
mallorymonroebooks.com
or
austinbrookpublishing.com
or
Amazon.com/author/mallorymonroe
for more information on all titles.